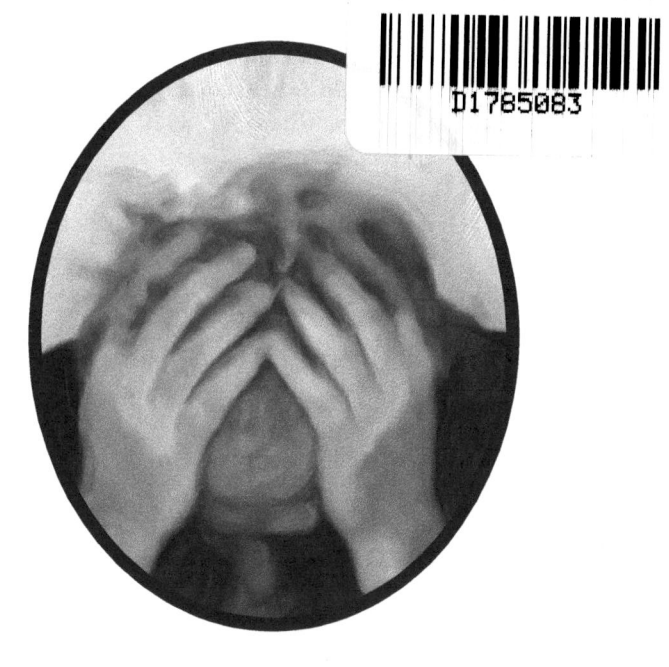

HEART FEVER

BOB VAN LAERHOVEN

ANAPHORA LITERARY PRESS

BROWNSVILLE, TEXAS

ANAPHORA LITERARY PRESS
1898 Athens Street
Brownsville, TX 78520
https://anaphoraliterary.com

Book design by Anna Faktorovich, Ph.D.

Printed in the United States of America, United Kingdom and in Australia on acid-free paper.

Published in 2018 by Anaphora Literary Press

Heart Fever
Bob Van Laerhoven—1st edition.

Library of Congress Control Number: 2017914844

Library Cataloging Information
Laerhoven, Bob Van, author.
   Heart fever / Bob Van Laerhoven
   114 p. ; 9 in.
   ISBN 978-1-68114-391-0 (softcover : alk. paper)
   ISBN 978-1-68114-392-7 (hardcover : alk. paper)
   ISBN 978-1-68114-393-4 (e-book)
1. Fiction—Mystery & Detective—Short Stories.
2. Fiction—Mystery & Detective—Historical.
3. Fiction—Thrillers—Psychological.
PN3311-3503: Literature: Prose fiction
840: French & related literatures

HEART FEVER

Bob Van Laerhoven

Acknowledgements

"The Abomination": first published in *Wasafiri* issue 83, autumn 2015.

"Paint it, Black": first published in *Brussels Noir*, Akashic Books, 2016.

The other three stories have not been in print before.

The Abomination

Roughly fifteen minutes to go before *Al-Thar*.

After the agony and humiliation of these last weeks, a clear certainty rules my head; revenge is the only honorable way out of this situation.

Barricaded here in this room, staring into the mirror I deliberately positioned in front of me, I address a mental message to my *khaal* Bashar al-Assad, ruler of Syria: 'Stand tall, revered uncle of every Alawite, hold out your arms, extend your *shabh* until your shadow covers every Syrian citizen, commanding them to obey you or die."

To the Westerners in this hospital and especially to the woman Quagebuur, I say, 'Fuck you and may you rot in hell.'

Allah ou akbar.

***

Ten minutes left, I figure.

Outside Amman shimmers in the sun, its pastel skyscrapers and hungry noises filling the window. In this light and at this moment, it could be the portal to *Akhirah*, the afterlife.

A pious part of me that came to life after the accident in Al-Houla whispers that I will be a true Muslim martyr.

I shall have my reward of servants and wives under the eternal dome adorned with pearls, aquamarine and ruby, as wide as the distance from Al-Jabiyyah to Sana'a.

An older part of me, the Wildman I have always been at heart, murmurs: 'I hope the *houris* in Paradise will be up to scratch. If they're virgins as the Prophet said, then they'll have a fucking lot to learn. To suck a man's dick right, for instance. Of course, I'll have eternity to teach them and, like all Muslim men in heaven, I'll be the equivalent of Adam, sixty cubits tall. Let's hope my dong will be in proportion.'

I look at the glass of whiskey in my left hand. I have always liked my booze strong and sinful.

I drain the glass. There's still enough for two more shots in the bottle.

That should do the trick.

Alcohol is a two-fanged demon; it sharpens my instincts, but it also jangles my memories.

The last thing I want to think about right now is that Belgian nurse, Quagebuur.

But I do.

***

'You've lost the will to live because your inflated ego and your macho frame of mind can't cope with what has happened to you,' she said in tolerable Arabic, the blunt Belgian woman, Veronique Quagebuur, head nurse here in this Doctors without Borders hospital, when the shrapnel had been removed from my legs and I could finally hobble around.

'You're also clinically depressed because your system needs steroids to make you feel like a man and you're not allowed them here. Your gonads are too small to restart the production of indigenous testosterone after years of steroid abuse. You're obsessed with the notion that your body is paperclip thin and weak. We have a medical term for that obsession—reverse anorexia.'

I was sitting in front of her in the hospital's bustling and noisy consultation area. *Your gonads are too small?*

If we had been alone, I would have snapped her neck with one arm for daring to speak to me like that. Her hair was tied up and she wasn't wearing a *niqab,* not even a scarf. A whore like that, with auburn hair and black eyes, questioning my manhood?

She leaned on her desk: 'For the record: were you one of the *Shabiha* in Syria? One of the Ghost Killers?'

We stared at each other, close together, worlds apart. The glassy sheen of disbelief in each other's eyes.

***

I could have told the Belgian woman that *Shabih* doesn't mean

Ghost. It's *Shabah*, plural *ashbah*. We're named after the Mercedes 600 we used for our raids— nickname *shabah*—and after the unique way—*tashbih*—we visit wrath upon others, those who are not Assadists.

We like to kill with the knife for our leader Bashar al-Assad, so everyone will know that it was the *Shabiha* who did it and everyone will know who is master in our motherland.

'We are Doctors without Borders,' Quagebuur continued when she realized I wasn't going to answer her question. 'In this hospital, aggressors and victims are treated the same. Sunnite, Shiite, Alawite, Christian, supporter of Assad's regime or rebel are notions that belong out there,' she pointed to the window, to the streets, 'not in here.'

My mouth remained closed. I had heard that pictures we had taken of each other with our smart phones had reached the Western press. Before I was brought here, I shaved my beard; an unmanly thing to do, but shrewd in these circumstances.

I had hoped it would be enough, but I couldn't hide my weight-lifter's body.

I continued trying to stare her down, as I had done many times with my blood brother Massab.

Her eyes were those of a dog: attentive and shiny. She didn't avoid my gaze, 'If you prefer to remain silent, that's fine with me, but you must know that your desire not to live anymore, which you expressed so clearly yesterday afternoon when our staff came to dress the wounds on your legs, is a symptom of severe depression. Your body, the sight of which filled others with fear, is damaged beyond repair and you can't stand it.'

I didn't react at all.

She sighed, her mouth a curve of disdain: 'Think about it, look into the mirror, and be honest with yourself.'

She picked up a pen, scribbled a few notes, stood up. Instead of leaving the room, she came and stood at my right shoulder. She bowed and whispered in my ear, 'If you don't like what you see in the mirror, what will you do?'

I looked over my shoulder and saw her eyes honing in on the stump that had once been my right arm; six weeks ago it had been sixty centimeters of muscle.

Bob Van Laerhoven

***

Eight minutes?

I look at myself as I wait, at the mirror, at what's left of me, just as the infidel Quagebuur asked me to.

She's a dumb cow. She spoke as if looking in a mirror were a punishment, worse, a humiliation..

What does she know?

Before I lost my arm and chunks of my legs, I liked to look in mirrors and see the monstrous strength in my pectorals, my shoulders, my torso, my legs, my arms.

Mirrors defined me.

I also liked ramming people's faces into mirrors, spattering blood, glass and tissue.

***

I remember looking at myself in the mirror at our gym, flexing my biceps, the right one tattooed with the face of sheikh Bashar al-Assad, and my friend Massab commenting: 'Rani, look at those biceps. You must be stronger than The Hulk by now. You are becoming The Abomination.'

The night before, in his apartment, Massab had put on a DVD of his favorite American movie, *The Incredible Hulk*. We drank the liquor Massab's brother-in-law had smuggled in from Jordan as we watched. Massab's apartment was a safe place to booze, given his reputation in the neighborhood for being a weapons freak. Entering his apartment without an invitation was a death sentence and everyone knew it, even our *mudir*, Shaheed Batala, the boss of our Alawite clan. We called him Night runner behind his back because of his appetite for young virgins. But even if Massab had been a peaceful man, Shaheed would not have interfered with the booze. He was convinced that drinking was but a minor sin in the eyes of Allah, the Almighty, and certainly forgivable for soldiers like us who had to fight the enemies of our country every day.

I had injected a cocktail of steroids a few hours earlier and the alcohol made me listless and numb, but I sat upright when The Abomination appeared on the screen. When the movie was over, I asked Massab to play it again.

And again.

The Abomination: a monster of muscle. A creature of destruction. Inspiring fear and awe.

Murderous and relentless. A towering presence, hard as a rock, stronger even than The Hulk, who's scared shitless when they fight. But *The Incredible Hulk* is an American movie; the measly Hulk wins in the end because Western infidels prefer emotional trash and inner turmoil to sheer strength and razor-sharp determination. The Hulk only wins the battle against The Abomination because he's cunning and sly, which is the mark of a coward. The Abomination is the stronger of the two; he would have won in a fair fight. He lost because he didn't do what it takes—fight with everything you can find.

We fought for victory over our enemies with everything we could find: guns, blades, clubs, and our bare hands.

In our region of Al-Nasiriyah, the people whispered behind our backs that we were meatheads, gangs of bandits with the brains of seven-year-olds.

They may have been right about some of us. But not about me.

I knew why I trained like a madman. We had to be colossal and let them see our bulging muscles in order to instill instant terror in the people on the streets. We Alawites are the natural superior race of all Muslims. Shaheed Batala formulated it like this: 'One Alawite is worth seven Shiites and seven Sunnites.'

So it's not only our duty, but also our right to defend the power of our *khaal* Bashar al-Assad with whatever it takes.

It's as simple as that.

Although it isn't easy; being powerful and superior is also a burden.

You always have to be on your guard. You always have to be the best.

That evening, I took the DVD of *The Incredible Hulk* home with me.

On my way I pictured myself as The Abomination and a sudden blast of carnal lust and longing for bloodshed surged through me, made the street reverberate and my teeth chatter.

Tomorrow, I thought, we cleanse the town of Al-Houla.

***

'It would be cool if I had The Abomination's spiky spine,' I joked when we were on the Tripoli Road heading for Al-Houla, remembering the first time I had seen *The Incredible Hulk*, gasping with delight when the super monster made its appearance. Knowing what we were about to do in Al-Houla, which families had been targeted for this raid, made me feel as if The Abomination lurked within me, waiting to morph me into its own shape.

Massab was sitting next to the driver of our SUV. He smiled and raised his smart phone to take a picture of me. It had become one of his favorite pastimes in recent months, since I had gained roughly two kilos of muscle every three weeks or so.

'When we're done in Al-Houla, you will definitely feel the first spikes growing,' he said quietly. Our eyes met in the rearview mirror.

'You may not be a superhero like The Abomination, but you have the look of a massive bear,' I said.

He was silent for a few minutes.

'A bear isn't powerful enough to tackle you,' he answered at last, flexing his right arm and looking at it. 'But before long I will be so big that even you will have to concede I am the strongest.'

I knew what he meant; for the last few days he had been taking gigantic doses of steroids in a single-minded attempt to be the strongest of all of us. There was already a rumor doing the rounds that it had cost him his manhood, but no one would dare mention it in his presence. Others whispered that his liver had 'the dimensions of a coconut.'

'That'll be the day,' I said. Our eyes met again.

Massab was the first to look away.

We turned into Satto Street where the Al-Hassan clan was waiting to join us.

When they saw us they lifted their weapons high in the air. We got out of the car to greet the elder of the clan.

My feet touched the ground when Massab drew his gun and put it to my temple. I stiffened. With his other hand he held out his smart phone to take our picture.

'Always remember that being the strongest doesn't make you invulnerable,' he said softly, and then, with a big smile:

'Happy hunting, brother!'

We laughed and kissed each other's bearded cheeks.

But I now knew that Massab carried the seed of jealousy, a weed that's almost impossible to destroy. It only grows in the heart, where we make all our important decisions.

***

In spite of the liquor and the drugs, I'm still convinced I'm a noble Muslim warrior and a robust defender of my clan.

The Qur'an says we should never kill, except to prevent the spread of corruption, and that was what we did. It takes a strong soul to cut a baby's throat, but if you don't have the guts to do it, you'll have to deal with a mortal enemy of your clan one day seeking revenge. When the Prophet emerged long ago from the Trench of War and laid down his sword, Gabriel appeared to him, shouting: 'Have you abandoned the fight? By Allah, the Angels have not yet put down their weapons. Go out and kill your enemies!'

We did exactly that. We did the Work of Angels.

'Don't think,' our *mudir* Shaheed Batala used to say. 'Act.'

Here in this hospital I have become a thinker. In the last three weeks, while the wounds on my legs healed, I read twenty-two installments of *The 99*, a comic series about superheroes, each with one of the powers of Allah, may his Name be blessed forever.

Teshkeel Publishing has done a nice job with this series, but I still miss the raw power of The Abomination. It made me think as I lay on my bed, brooding, still trying to cope with a missing arm and not being able to walk.

In *The 99*, the good heroes always win.

It's the will of Allah, His name be Praised.

In the Holy Qur'an, Allah the All Glorious ordains what has to be done to our enemies: 'Smite ye above their necks and smite all their finger-tips of them.'

All infidels, who are our natural enemies, should be treated that way.

But also Muslims who rebel against their lawful sheikh are to be treated as enemies.

So that's what we did.

Conclusion: we were the good heroes.

Why then did this terrible thing happen to me?

The thought came to me as a revelation; my wounds were a trial, willed by Allah Himself. He wanted me to overcome this horror and win in the end.

Allah wanted me to win a meaningful victory, one that I could offer in honor of his Name.

At that moment, lying on my hospital bed and staring at the stump of my right arm, I made my vow.

***

When our enemies in Al-Houla saw me and my gang coming, they knew they were doomed. Instead of putting up a fight, the families that had been picked for extermination cowered in their houses and did nothing to resist us when we slit their throats, men, women and children alike. We shouted at them to fight back, we poked them with our weapons to arouse their anger. Their chicken-livered behavior disgruntled us. A woman hiding under the sheets of her bed like a big hump of clay; I tore her *nijab*, unveiled her. She stared at me in shock. I thrust my pistol into her hand, invited her to take a shot at me. At that moment, seized by the spirit of Allah the Avenger, I sincerely thought I was invincible. She cowered; the pistol fell to the floor. I laughed. She was very young and tender, so I did what warriors do when their prey is female and afterwards I shot her gently in the head instead of cutting her throat.

Was I drunk? High? Both?

I didn't know anymore. For me, it felt like we were levitating, floating above the ground. The world was no longer a place of humans, but seemed connected with spirit beings that flew in and out of our bodies as they wished. Their fangs became our fangs; their red-tinted eyes our eyes.

The evening before the attack on Al-Houla, Massab had told me that when you toss a body out of a window five storeys up, its eyeballs pop out. I didn't believe him and called him the Superhero of Fantasy.

He looked at me in his usual peculiar way.

***

Six storeys high in an apartment building near the local Baath

Party headquarters in Al-Houla. Massab and I racing up the stairs, shouting *Allah ou Akbar* at the top of our voices. The father of the targeted family came to us with a bribe, pleading and wailing. We shot him in the belly. There were others, but there was a mist in front of my eyes. I don't recall if they were grown-ups or children.

But I clearly remember the boy wriggling in Massab's grip.

'I'll show you it's true!' he bellowed and I immediately knew what he meant. He hurried to the window and tossed the boy out into the shimmering air as if he were a sack of garbage.

Next: Massab and I outside the apartment building, turning over the remains of the boy who had fallen face down onto the pavement.

We stared wide-eyed. 'I win!' shouted Massab. He grabbed me by the arm, excited, shook it. I felt his pride and his jealousy towards me burn like a furnace.

I yanked at him, he fell against the wall.

I pointed my right arm at him. I didn't know what I wanted to say to him, the words stuck in my throat like fish bones.

A high-pitched sound. A blast.

My arm swelled to inhuman proportions in front of my eyes and then disappeared.

Massab's face became a blur of red.

His arterial blood spattered all over me.

***

We had been hit by friendly fire, Shaheed told me later. It was an accident. We had to abort the raid because a gang of rebels had entered Al-Houla. They outnumbered us. Shaheed examined me in the SUV where they'd dumped me.

'You need medical care fast or you're going to bleed to death.'

They left me in Taldou, where a delegation from Doctors without Borders was setting up a field hospital. I was later transferred to the central hospital in Amman.

What can I say? It's *Taqdir*, the Fate bestowed on me by Allah. For He created us to worship Him and obey Him.

This world is no more than a test.

Allah has seen fit to test me to my limits and beyond.

It's as Quagebuur said: Doctors without Borders treat both the aggressors and the aggressed. No distinctions.

They think they're doing the right thing.

They couldn't be more wrong.

***

Six minutes.

Or less.

It was the endless whining of the little girl in the room opposite that really set me on my path to *Al-Thar*. She moaned and screeched day and night like an *ifriti* or a *zar*, those ghosts my mother used to tell me about that haunt women and children. I endured the howling for days on end, demanding more painkillers, dreaming about the steroid cocktails I used to take: Stanozolol, Deca Durabolin, Dianabol, Winstrol. The feeling they gave me; as if my body was about to burst at the seams, my veins bulging from the pressure they built up in my muscles and organs. I noticed that I indulged certain fantasies when I took huge loads of steroids combined with speed. They lasted a long time and triggered crazy scenes in my head of me ripping people apart, attacking and devouring wild animals, slaying powerful fantasy creatures.

In hindsight, my fantasies were the real stuff of superhero comics, not the kids' stuff of *The 99*.

We regularly used speed when we were out on patrol. As a result, time seemed endless, obstacles puny. We could go on for days, but after a long raid exhaustion would hit me like the blow of a hammer. The weariness it brought made me feel as if the hellish Pit of Infidels mentioned in the Holy Qur'an had materialized in my gut. At those times, in those last moments before sleep, still fearing that this shroud would never lift, I thought of my mother.

She worshipped me.

She called me her little prince.

She would egg me on when I was sick, which happened often in my youth, tell me I had to do more than the other boys to grow strong. *And one day*, she said, *you will lift mountains.*

At those moments, when my mind was slack and my self-control had frayed at the edges, I sometimes felt wetness on my cheeks.

I haven't given a single thought to my mother while I've been here in the hospital.

Until now.

I look away from the mirror. I touch my cheeks.

They're dry.

***

Six days ago, I filled the doorway of the room opposite, staring at the girl, irritated beyond reason by her endless moaning.

Before I could say a word, I recognized her.

She had been in the house in al-Houla that had burst into flames after a couple of grenade explosions.

One from Massab. One from me.

I approached the bed. Her left cheek had been eaten away by fire.

Her hands too.

It was then that Quagebuur appeared behind me. 'They're preparing her for a skin transplant. It takes a lot of time. And for her, a lot of pain.'

Her voice, as usual, seemed self-assured, but now there was a hint of something else. A note of accusation?

Of pity?

I looked down at the woman and, to my own surprise, I was silent.

What do stupid Westerners know about the honor of hatred?

The honor of following a *caliph*, a civil and religious leader like Bashar al-Assad, to the death?

I shook my head and showed her my teeth.

At that moment the child cried out again. A gurgling sound followed by a high pitched wail.

Quagebuur said in that irritating voice of hers: 'Her chin and tongue are severely burned. Her mother, father and two sisters were murdered.'

The child opened her eyes and looked at me.

She recognized my moon-shaped face—my mother called me 'moonface'—I could see it in her eyes. I had always had a puffy face. The steroids only made it more pronounced. Even without my beard, she knew who I was. I came closer. She cowered, tried to hide.

She was so afraid that, at last, she fell silent. I smiled and touched her hair.

We had cut her father's throat while she was weeping in a corner.

We had stabbed her mother in the belly, again and again, yelling that she was a whore.

We had crushed the tiny skulls of her two sisters with the butts of our AK-47s.

It was then that our brothers had come under attack and called for our help.

We ran from the house, each of us tossing in a grenade to finish her off.

The little girl in the corner.

***

Day after day I would visit the girl's bed when she was crying and making the life of the other patients miserable.

Inevitably, she fell silent when she saw me.

I always stroked her hair with my remaining hand. Sometimes, I would sit on her bed for hours.

We would stare at each other. She never said a word.

Nor did I.

Her eyes said everything. Her silence was a blessing.

***

Two minutes.

Funny.

In the end, it was for the girl's sake that I decided to blow up this wretched hospital.

Wherever I went in this place I saw people staring at my mutilated legs and missing arm, but most of all I wanted to end her river of tears.

Her weeping reminded me of *Mubram*, humanity's inevitable destiny.

Our destiny is suffering.

As if indeed we are the People in the Pit of Hell.

They said I was a dumb ox and Massab too.

You don't have to be smart to do what I did. You just need the training.

An hour ago, at lunch time, I went into the pharmacy of the

hospital, slammed the pharmacist's head against the wall and barricaded the door. All I needed was an undisturbed hour and some
aspirin, which I purified with warm acetone. Then, as I had been
taught, I mixed sulphuric acid and potassium nitrate into the acetyl-
salicylic acid. I had fifteen grams of ASA and I ended up with fifteen
grams of picric acid, a highly explosive homemade bomb. I placed
the device near the hospital's supply of ethanol used for cleaning.

I look in the mirror.

Any second now.

The Weeper, as I call the little girl, will be better off. My arms
were sixty centimeters in circumference.

I truly was The Abom—

First Published in: *Wasafiri*, Vol. 30, No. 3, September 2015, pp. 45-49.
Print ISSN: 0269-0055, online ISSN: 1747-1508.

Abducted and Raped by Aliens

2011

*L*ooky-Looky, the NY-night is bitter like worm-seed and cold as a cop demanding, *legitimize yourself.* This NY-night is a flying saucer-night. Even when they don't fly, the imagination does. Looky-Looky, a yellow-glossed imagination glides by on four wheels with a Puerto Rican behind the wheel, blowing pink bubblegum bubbles, transporting a slightly drunk Belgian/Flemish writer to a gathering of UFO-abductees. On the phone, Stanislas Nakowski was saying euphorically: "Great stuff for my new book, Penman! Far-out! Gotta see this, man! One of the bitches is a *tenner*! A first-class nut-case to boot!"

In the taxi, Penman sits brooding over his first meeting, in 1999, with Stanislas Nakowski, now a best-selling author, then an over-active speed junk, an *earnalist* from *USA Today,* for the first time dipping his toes in a war-zone, in Kükes, Kosovo.

Penman hums: "*So tonight I'm gonna party like it's nineteen ninety-nine.*"

He gazes at the NY-brownstones, bridges, metal and malls. This is a night for the imagination to transmogrify—wow, a word that wobbles the wee imagination—NYC into a silver disk of opportunities to become a millionaire.

Penman's imagination grumbles and growls, *I'm on strike.*

This was not the case with Stanislas Nakowksi's Muse when he wrote *Abducted and Raped by Aliens,* a high-strung tale about aliens popping up at random in people's bedrooms to abduct them and to inspect their bodies in full detail in a whirl of nauseating UFO-lights. The abductees would have sex with aliens in utmost kinky ways.

So, this is the situation, according to Penman: after having published more than 30 elitist novels in Flanders—why, of all places, has

Fate pushed him through the birth tunnel in *Flanders?*—he is still as poor as a louse, while Stanislas, with his lousy imitation of a brain, has published one book and became rotten rich.

Penman's *phonehome* blares.

It's Stanislas, asking when Penman will arrive. The abductees he's visiting tonight for a follow-up of his bestseller are pretty impatient. It's barely their third meeting and already the Belgian/Flemish author is going to visit! "I've told them you're waaaaaay famous in Belgium,'" Stanislas croaks.

"They're cooked up! Hurry! Hop hop hop!"

Shit, Penman thinks, *only in Eeeeeennnn Waaaaay Seeeeeeeee do you meet the most incredible madmen, freaking out like only NYC-bananas can.*

***

He gets out of the taxi in front of a Brownsville brownstone. Wild neighborhood, son, oh yeah. Echoes in the stair hall, steel wired doors in the lift, an apartment door opening. There he is, his arms outstretched for a huge hug, the one and only Stanislas Nakowski, the UFO-writer, son of a Jewish father with Russian roots and a Brazilian black mother. Milk-chocolate skin, small, but with an almost feminine bottom. As if they had seen each other yesterday, Stanislas yells, "Dear Pen, come in! After all these years! You haven't changed a hair!"

"You neither, my friend, great to see you." *Shit,* Penman thinks. *Skin wrinkled like an old turd. And that coyote-look in his eyes. Revved up again! Like in the old days in Kosovo.*

The Flemish author smiles a big Flemish smile and shakes hands, while discreetly eyeballing the worn-out living-room and the people in it.

Theresa: a mulatto with sharply etched facial features, and a nice glow on her skin, but with a Burgundian ass and dropsy legs, which she shows the world in a perky, way too short skirt.

Nathalie: a slender woman with luxurious brown hair and altogether an alluring, almost boyish frame propped up by traffic stopping boobies.

Chaim: Nathalie's husband, a Sephardic Jew without a *kippah* and with Italian looks, but behold those rubber lips and sly eyes: beware!

Terrence: Theresa's boy-friend, a big-boned black man with a prominent nose, a good-natured smile, and a scar on his left cheek.

No alien in sight.

***

Drinks. Salted snacks. A kitchen with a ferociously vibrating re-frigerator. It doesn't take long for Penman to smoke the calumet with Stanislas and the abductees.

Shit, a particular set of half-soles. But their ganja is superb.

Almost ceremonial, Penman unpacks his old-fashioned tape-re-corder—no digital, fancy stuff for him, *blech*—punches a few knobs and declares the group interview ready to launch.

Encouraged by Penman's pontifical gaze, Nathalie, shifting restless on a sofa with a *Beavis and Butthead* print, explains that *grays*—a pecu-liar race of aliens on the dark side of *E. T.*—have raped her for years with huge raptor and that they can't be stopped because other people simply don't see them. The *grays* invariably follow the same pattern: Nathalie wakes up after a horrible dream, and when she looks around, bathing in sweat and with palpitations that make her ribcage shudder—"like this, see?"—she feels that she's not alone in the room. The *grays* materialize from the walls and surround her bed. Nathalie tries to wake up Chaim, but her husband snores on, without moving a finger. When she prods him, it's like touching a dead fish—*blech.*

Without mercy or compassion, the *grays* transport her. *Flop*, sud-denly she's lying on a table in a space ship—like in virtual reality, dig? Pinpricks of light everywhere, a pulsating ceiling, humming, like ritual singing. A cloaked *insectoid* inserts a needle in her belly. It doesn't hurt; it angers Nathalie, in spite of her fear. The *insectoid* is assisted by a *gray* who, by means of telepathy, explains to Nathalie that this ex-periment is necessary. The aliens want to harvest the cells of her body. Afterwards, a naked humanoid enters the scene. He has a long, dark and thin "genital organ" that "seems brittle, and not a single hair on his body." He "copulates" with Nathalie, and, it must be said, he's marvel-ously skillful, although not once does he blink an eye.

Rhythmic like a pinball-machine, the humanoid pushes/pushes/pushes. He goes on for so long that Nathalie gets dizzy. The whole af-fair becomes more nauseating than a roller coaster, dig?

And then the humanoid....

Nathalie stops, rolls her eyes. She bends over and produces retching noises. Stanislas bounces off the sofa. "This is what so often happens with abductees! The *grays* have inserted a deeply hidden posthypnotic suggestion in her brain that keeps her from telling *in detail* what they did to her!"

The vibe in the room is razor-sharp.

Post-hypnotical suggestion, my ass, Penman thinks. *Stanislas is as crazy as a Cracow.*

Penman pens like mad in his little notebook—very old-fashioned, but that's Penman's way of doing things.

Lo and behold: the show is beyond his expectations. Nathalie falls back in the sofa, bumps her belly up and starts mooing rather offensively.

Penman jots down inexplicable notes in his *carnet,* "What's the deal here? The alien hides in all of us and keeps us imprisoned in his flying saucer-bubble." Also inexplicably, our Flemish author all of a sudden remembers his many relationships that were broken by inexplicable desires, inexplicable orientations, and inexplicable fears.

The emotional wave ends with a magnanimous pity for the inexplicable people around him.

Chaim tries in vain to block the others' view on Nathalie's panties. Stanislas delves into his rucksack and produces a small mirror and silver-colored vials. With delicious agility, he stuffs a significant amount of coke in Nathalie's blowholes. The coke *cokes* in overdrive: Nathalie's eyes become glassy and content. "When she's like that, this procedure is the sole thing that can calm her down," Stanislas explains. The other abductees produce consenting sounds. Stanislas asks his European guest if the usage of a "prohibited substance" is a culture shock for him.

It isn't.

Ah, so maybe he also wants some?

Penman blinks and sniffs a line, maladroit and jerkily like a dog suspiciously sniffing a treat. *Whoa,* gratis coke and a decent view on Nathalie's resilient body lying on the sofa, her legs indecently spread, enjoying circumstantial coke-rigors.

In a shy voice, Terrence asks if it wouldn't be better if Stanislas first showed their guest the video-recording. Bouncy as ever, Stanislas jumps up and starts a videotape. Meanwhile he explains that a few months ago, the group installed a video-camera in Chaim's and Nathalie's bedroom.

Twenty days later: bingo.

Invasion.

Looky-Looky, Penman feels *très ému* when he sees the two sleeping bodies of Chaim and Nathalie, snoring under a ridiculous silver-metal baldachin. The image on the screen is reasonably clear. The blinds of the bedroom window are partly closed and magical NY-pinpricks of light dance inside. *Tadààm*: the image becomes fuzzy, shadows *cavort* through the room.

Penman suspects a fraud: misty images, fuzzy background, clumsy shapes as if someone is swinging toy bears around.

Grays, my ass, Penman thinks. At that very moment, a creature rushes to the camera, a head becomes visible in a flash: sharp beak, big black eyes, thin nose—more like two holes in leathery skin—no mouth.

Heehaw, Penman thinks. *The carnival-mud head of service.*

The image disintegrates into grey pixels.

Stanislas declares pompously that, "for unknown reasons," the camera stopped recording, but worked perfectly the morning after. From the look of him, Chaim seems mightily impressed, although he undoubtedly has seen the recording many times before. With his head in his hands, rocking to and fro as if he's reciting in front of Jerusalem's Wailing Wall, he starts muttering a mantra. Penman edges closer to him and hears, "She's doing it for the sex." Penman sighs deep in his bowels. High as a chicken, for sure, that husband of a doubtless meganeurotic wife.

A goody-goody rush hits him in the stomach.

Oh, wow, yeah man, getting *slizzard.*

Suddenly, Chaim raises his head and roars, "She's doing it for the sex!"

This seems to trigger his wife. Nathalie struggles out of the sofa, pulls down the hem of her skirt and yells, gesturing as if she's a prima donna in a classical opera, "Sex is danger! Sex lures you into the flying saucer!"

Penman loses it and screams, "The flying *saucisse*! (Bratwurst)" Bleating, he falls from the sofa, meanwhile thinking, *Damn good stuff, this coke. I'm making a grandiose fool of myself, but I'm having a ball. I also teach them some French, the lucky bastards.*

"My psychotherapist tells me that I'm too goal-orientated in matters of sex," Chaim confesses miserably.

"You can't get me fucking off!" Nathalie chirps.

Chaim throws a cushion at her. One of the tips hits Nathalie in the left eye. She makes a lot of impolite noises, kicks dreadnought a small side table standing between her and her husband out-of-the-way, and assumes an impressive Kung Fu-stance. Tears smear the make-up under her left eye.

Penman, still on the floor, watches the scene topsy-turvy, and notices that Nathalie is wearing very frivolous panties indeed. She yodels an Indian war-cry, and attacks her yokemate.

Penman scrambles up, ready to mediate, but loses his equilibrium, and falls against Nathalie's back. Chaim interprets this move as a violation of Nathalie's privacy, a thing not taken lightly by Americans.

The trio drops in a wrestling tangle on the floor when the front door bell rings. Terrence, wide-eyed and stunned by the scene, opens it on the assumption that the rest of the abductees' club has arrived.

He receives a blow on his nose-bridge with a Sig Sauer, and collapses against the wall. Two men wearing track suits and masks rush into the flat. Holy Cow—home-hacking—a fearful NYC-phenomenon, usually carried out by junkies. This time, it's different: we're dealing with foot-soldiers of Mr. Plaurent "Lenti" Dervishaj, whose NYC-organization manages all crime-jobs imaginable. These men dwell on the bottom of the food-chain, and have to start *somewhere* and *somehow* to climb up the ladder.

The home-hackers holler that they want loot. Although his limbs shudder from an adrenaline rush, Penman recognizes their accent. *Albanians?*

The first one rounds up the group. Penman gets hit on the head for being too slow. The apartment tilts, he's lying with his back on the floor again, it's becoming a habit. The impact of the blow has twisted his head aside. Through a haze, he sees how Nathalie, who's still floored, fiddles in her bag beside her.

Penman looks up in frog-perspective and gets a clear view of the first home-hacker's mask.

It is a rubber mug, resembling exactly the *gray* he has just seen on the video-tape.

Olalla, can't be coincidence, is without a doubt an evocative literary metaphor!

Or else a sign that the videotape is rigged, falsified, faked, and bogus.

Nathalie pulls a small gun out of her handbag.

Turmoil/turmoil/turmoil: that's why the home-hackers don't pay attention to the armed woman on the floor.

Nathalie points her gun with two hands.

Nathalie shoots.

And keeps on shooting until the magazine is empty.

NY-violence! Rawer than a raw steak! Hotter than *Reservoir Dogs*!

Lots of deafening noises.

One of these noises is Nathalie's voice. "Never, never in the flying saucer again!"

Penman crawls to his feet. The rancid cordite-stench draws phlegm from all his breath-holes.

Blindly, he stumbles over bodies to the flat's balcony. Behind him, the screaming, yelling, and pleading, reaches an astonishing crescendo. Penman looks up, ever so slowly, to the heavens above NYC, the black skyline resembling the lining of an old magician's hat.

He looks briefly over his shoulder.

Sees Stanislas writhing on the carpet.

Remembers what the man said, 13 years ago, in Kükes, Albania.

When he got shot.

Writhing, bleeding, gurgling, hallucinating, the American had whispered in Penman's ear: "Beam me up. Please, Scotty, beam me up."

1998

In the wild, wild east, let go of the beast.

Penman could find nothing more streetwise than this crippled rhyme, intimidated as he was by the presence of Stanislas Nakowski, American star reporter for *USA Today* in Kükes, Kosovo-Albania—no, this double-fanged nationality is not a mistake, folks: parts of Kükes were Albanian territory, other parts Kosovar.

Nakowski was a mulatto who stuck out in the pale press-crowd like a red parasol in a sea of white.

Penman, a constantly broke Belgian free-lance travel writer, envied Stanislas Nakowski's endless resources. USA Today, *hey hey hey!* No wonder that Nakowski's attitude was regal. He was a 100 kilogauss women's magnet, *yessirree.*

Producers and TV-hosts from the four corners of the Earth had come tumbling down in Kükes, wearing their cocky battledresses, luring the local female translators with their microphones and camera's until they engaged in sex with consent.

Penman possessed not even an inch of a battle dress. He was a *Flemish* writer, you see, and all Flemish writers were tramps, or worse, *yak*. At night, trying to sleep in the stinking hallway of a drafty apartment, rented for a barbarian sum, Penman's heart pounded noisily with lust and fear, alternating on the rhythm of the Serbian mortars shelling the region.

Kükes harbored a lot of *hakmurrje*. This *über*ghost of blood feuds was so hungry that, at night, it howled like a crazed mountain wind.

On nights like that, Penman brooded over the fact that life wasn't fair.

On top of that, life wasn't pretty either. In the mornings, when producers and TV-anchors slurped their coffee in café-bar-hotel *Ammerika* with their pretty female translators, who clearly suffered from back pains, the illustrious duo Windblown Dreams and Stampeding Ambitions roamed the dining room.

Hunger, physical and psychical, ruled Penman.

***

Zoom in.

Stanislas Nakowski sat at the breakfast table and disdainfully gnawed on a bone-hard croissant, smeared with moldy jam. At his side: not a local female translator, but Katie, bitchy-bitchy reporter from *The Sun,* the UK-tabloid of tabloids. Stanislas was fashionably drab: unwashed teeth, greasy curls, drowsy eyes, a real star reporter in war-conditions. The *muzak* in café-bar-hotel *Ammerika* went like this: *that's the way to do it, money for nothin' and yur chicks for free...*

Katie suffered from back-pain. She stumbled to the toilet. Stanislas informed Penman casually that he had done her yesterday, done her real good, FTW, damn *kiff*.

It was something real men did in real war-conditions.

Katie's face was ugly as a turnip—dixit Stanislas—but she flaunted a five-star-body, and possessed mountainous sexual energy.

Half an hour later, Katie from the *Sun* turned out—dixit Penman—to be a nice woman who laughed her lungs to pieces with the moronic articles she had to write for the *Sun.*

Stanislas had to pull out. He had paid a shit-load of *baksheesh* to an informant who would introduce him to a branch of the Kosovo Liberation Army (KLA). This would assure a five-star-feature in *USA Today*, no Gwen Stefani about it.

Penman possessed infinite small-currency of *baksheesh*-money, and a magnitude of time while Katie from *The Sun* was a beginner, so they strolled together through Kükes, and enjoyed the local tourism potential: the muddy streets, postmodern garbage piles, endless tractor-caravans, walking scarecrows, looming assassins, sneaking hooligans, teeth-gnashing *hakmurrje*-addicts, and simpleton kids.

Katie was delighted. The tales she would be able to tell in her favorite pub back home, *yodiddely*…

"This is oh so stale," she mumbled continuously.

"Yeah, stale," Penman replied, ogling the curve of her left mammary, D-cup-curvy, *yodiddely*…

Real men in real war-time had to ogle hooters, part of the job.

Katie ventilated some "oh so stale" theories about *The Refugee* in the 20th century, and confessed to having read the French philosopher Bernard-Henry Lévy, who had drooled a myriad of very French books about the subject.

Penman cut her short. "Bullshit. This is the century of *hakmurrje*. There is nothing more to it."

Katie started to think that Penman was a real man in real war-time.

Inch by inch, their heads came closer together. They hardly had an eye left for the refugees drifting through Kükes, not even for the old crones, sitting on a plastic sheet that barely insulated them from the icy mud covering the market-place. Penman nearly kicked one of them a double hernia. Attentively Katie pulled him aside just in time. Penman fell against her right breast tissue, and immediately bounced back.

The power of that mighty *boobie*: wow, holy cow.

Proud of having rescued Penman, and feeling wholesome warmth in her right breast, Katie didn't notice the young woman striding purposely up to her. When she saw her, it was too late. The blonde slapped her in the face, and hissed in a heavy accented English, "You don't deserve him, you ugly cunt!" She turned and marched away, her head held high, yelling in Kosovo-tongue at the people surrounding them.

Katie blushed daintily, stroked her cheek. There was already a crowd gathering, and a lot of shouting in even wilder Kosovo-tongue was going on. Unsavory characters began to push closer.

"This can become nasty," Penman said. He took Katie by the shoulders, and, without looking anyone in the eye, cleared a path.

He released his breath—*pufferthepuf*—when café-bar-hotel *Ammerika* came in sight.

Penman strutted out his chest and asked Katie if she wanted to open a can of beer with him.

***

After three cans of ridiculously expensive German lager, Katie confessed that the unshaved Kosovars terrified her with their raptor gazes, their nimble-fingered children, their Mister-Magic attitude, and their ragged rags.

"And their hot-headed women," Penman drily remarked.

Katie rubbed her swollen cheek. "She was a translator for Stanislas. He fired her."

"What was that entire vernacular about?"

"I haven't got a clue."

"Did she sleep with him, and reckons you're a competitor?" Penman noticed how formal his question was. It was a token that he was getting involved and he didn't want that.

 His will was frugal.

"He believes in aliens, you know. UFO's."

"Who?"

"Stanislas. And he's a tantric-master…You know…In bed."

"I know what Tantra is…It's just that…"

"What?"

"He doesn't seem the type."

Katie threw him an appraising glance. Penman found it inappropriate and provocative.

"He can go on for hours."

Penman's smile was tight. "Must hurt after a while."

His insight surprised her. She fiddled with her glass.

"I'm tired and a bit drunk," she said.

Silence. What to say? *Tantra here, tantra there, tantra everywhere?* Or maybe: *unsightly turnip head; five-star body?*

Katie reached a decision and demurely suggested that, in order for her to feel safe, Penman better accompany her, as a real *cavalier seul,* to her room.

***

In war-time, flashes flash *quicky-quicky* between Billy-goat and nanny-goat, also, if necessary between nanny-nanny and billy-billy.

Some ten minutes later, Penman and Katie from *The Sun* were hopping, nude as freshly shorn poodles, on the rickety bed in her room. Outside, *Lada* car-horns beeped, refugees exchanged refugee-talk, and tractor gear-boxes went crunch/crunch/crunch.

Penman meandered in Katie from *The Sun* like a fish on dry land, but he felt that she was thinking of Stanislas. For sure, she projected Stanislas' long eye-lashes and tawny skin on his pig-white, freckle-dotted hide.

Comecomecome, Katie panted.

The door opened.

Stanislas Nakowski barged in.

Katie produced a ghastly scream.

***

Expecting a Homeric fight between two billy goats?

So sorry to disappoint. It appeared that Stanislas was freaking out because, an hour earlier, standing on a mountain top, he had ogled a refugee convoy slipping down a mountain-road, and occasionally losing a vehicle in the ravines that crisscrossed the landscape.

That's how vehicles go in war-time.

A hailstorm had broken loose, weaving brown-red and yellow strings of light against the background of the raw, misty mountains.

By Jove, Stanislas saw how the yellow strings moved apart and dived like hawks toward the convoy. When a crash seemed inevitable, the yellow dots, changing into blinding white disks, had shot back with incredible speed into the skies.

Stanislas spat serious spittle: UFO's! Aliens!

"You should go easy on those speed-balls of yours," Penman said, pulling up his underpants. "Who knows what the Kosovars put in it? Drain-cleaner, I heard."

"Quite true." Katie closed her bra. "One of your Kosovo sluts just hit me in the face. She probably stole some of your speed-balls."

Penman wondered why Stanislas didn't show any fornication-wrath. *That's because of her troglodyte face,* he thought. Same old song:

the leftovers, the crumbs, the discarded goods were left to him.

Stanislas didn't comment on the Kosovo slut-thingy. He moved jerkily around the room, apparently unaware of their meantime semi-clothed condition. "I wasn't the only one who gawked the spectacle! My guide, Gotuz, saw them too! And not for the first time. Gotuz claims that strange phenomenon dwell regularly in the old subterranean city, underneath Kükes."

Katie and Penman gawked each other.

Yep.

Same old song.

Poor quality speed.

***

But you know how it is, between friends in war-time. After a few tedious days, they got bored and restless. There was not enough shooting lately, only now and then at night when drunken KLA-warriors pointed their Kalashnikov at the starry sky for a joyous salvo and hoarse damnations of the Serbians who didn't even deserve to be called cockroaches.

Therefore—and because Stanislas kept whining that at least they should visit the underground city for the thrill of the atmosphere alone—they gave in.

I am afraid of depths, Penman thought when the decision, sprinkled with precious cans of German lager, had been reached. *And now that I think about it, also of heights. And of the KLA. UFO's too. Yeah, well, of life, actually.*

The day before he had spotted a car with a Belgian plate, loaded with stocky individuals in battle dress and red KLA shoulder epaulets. Belgian Kosovars, true patriots coming to help their brethren!

Penman had knocked on the window. Bearded faces behind the glass, eyes like collar studs. One of them rolled the back window down. "Belgian Press!" Penman said. "Men, a statement for the Belgian home front of the immigrated Kosovars!"

"Hark ye, grapeless critter," was the answering growl in a guttural West-Flemish dialect. "No comment! Top secret!" The car accelerated, almost crushing Penman's right foot. He jumped back, got rammed by a passing moped, and toppled into the cold Kükes-mud.

With his nose drenched in prehistorically smelling sludge, Penman's mind-machine became lyrical: *this wet and slimy cold invading my nostrils is the swamp-stench of animal sex, eternal sex, war-sex.*

During the last few days, Stanislas, a bit too drugged to Penman's taste, had become obsessed by *alien sex.*

***

Penman kept his gaze on Stanislas' back. It looked quite untrustworthy in the tiny beam of Gotuz Kola's quite untrustworthy flashlight, quivering downwards.

Katie from *The Sun* was jabbering in the haunting darkness that was waiting beneath them like a pool of tar.

Gotuz Kola, basking in his memories of the glorious Albanian past of the eighties, wherein dictator Hoxha constructed under each city in greater Albania—Kükes had been an Albanian city in that era—a gigantic, water-dripping, concrete-rotting complex of shelters.

The shelters would guarantee Albanian victory when the inevitable Third World War exploded.

Precisely 184 steps beneath the surface, they reached ground level.

Sniffed the smell of fungi and stagnant water.

Corridors spread like a spider web, painted in purulent camouflage green.

Instinctively, Gotuz, Penman, Katie and Stanislas huddled closer together.

Above them: layers of silent earth.

Beneath them: more layers of silent earth.

"Immoral," Penman said.

"Interesting," Stanislas said. He giggled. "Where are the aliens?"

"These tunnels stink of mice, *blech*," Katie said.

"The Great Albanian people are invincible and will unite Albania and Kosovo!" Gotuz said.

Where are the fucking aliens? Stanislas thought. *For sure, the bastards have cloaked themselves!*

She has killer legs, Penman thought. *But what a mud duck melon. Such a shame.*

Light in different colors exploded, followed by bobbing shadows.

Mallkuar!* [* *Damn!*]

No way!

Mammy!

Damn the speed/Get away from the alien heat!
A low voice erupted from one of the tunnels.

It barked in an apish, growling, West-Flemish dialect: "'ye Beard of the Prophet, there you have that lard-ass from Belgium again!"

***

"Phew! Wow!" Stanislas jumped up and down on his seat in the white UNHCR-Land Rover that Gotuz Kola had secured via foggy international agencies to drive the American star reporter to all kinds of war-atrocities.

Stanislas turned around, faced Penman, who sat on the back seat next to Katie who was staring out of the window.

"What a story! We're goddamn lucky they recognized you, Pen. Fucking Christ! Who knows what they would've done if you hadn't been a Belgian reporter, a compatriot..." Stanislas shook his head.

Penman tried to radiate superior indifference.

"I wonder what they were doing down there. Holy Cowly Fuck!"

"I wouldn't go back if I was you," Penman said.

Stanislas shook his head again. "Oh boy, oh boyo..."

They drove in silence toward Kükes' center. Gotuz Kola made delicate though excessive use of the car horn to chase pedestrians out-of-the-way.

Stanislas looked out of the window when he said, as if to himself: "Donjeta claims she's pregnant. From me."

"Who is Donjeta?" Katie asked. There was a hint of triumph, of *appetite,* in her voice.

"You know who she is. She slapped you."

Gotuz Kola swung with an athletic turn into the street leading to café-bar-hotel *Ammerika.*

"What are you going to do about it?"

"I told her to find something else to swindle dough from."

"Did she slap you?" Katie said.

"I should be careful if I was you," Penman said. "These are vengeful hordes."

Stanislas shrugged.

A thin sound, like a bird-cry. The windshield cracked into a myriad of sharp-fangled stars.

Blood drops shot like tiny projectiles from Stanislas' left temple.

Gotuz Kola floored the accelerator.

2011

It's getting cold on the NYC-balcony.

Penman can't summon the strength to look over his shoulder and confront the havoc behind his back.

What sounds reach his dreamy ears? Groans? Sighs? Jelps of raptor?

What thoughts reach his computing synapses?

Is this a coke-dream?

Penman feels he isn't here. He isn't *in the now.*

The tiny blood drops from Stanislas' left temple so many years ago have blinded him.

It turned out to be a grazing shot.

By the next day, *USA Today* evacuated Stanislas. The newspaper hired a seat in a C-130 Hercules and waited impatiently for his story about his narrow escape from a war-hero's death in some backward region of Europe.

Stanislas had asked Penman not to mention to anyone the true reason for his war-wound. *Some hot-headed relatives from Donjeta... You know how those Balkan brutes are...*

English colleagues spirited Katie away. They wanted to explore the rumor that Kosovar-Albanian farmers had been executed by Serbian special forces in the hills an hour's drive from Kükes.

Katie vowed to Penman that she would be in touch.

She wasn't.

Totally disgusted with himself and the world, Penman hitched a ride on a MSF-convoy to the Albanian capital of Tirana, where he boarded a plane to the Brussels Airport.

Stanislas had also vowed to Penman that he would be in touch.

He was.

Until he touched gold with *Abducted and Raped by Aliens.*

Whereupon Penman got in touch with him.

***

"Beam me up. Please, Scotty, beam me up," Penman whispers.

Out of the blue and the black, like the lining of an old magician's hat, he starts to cry.

He sheds bitter tears for Katie from *The Sun,* whom he hasn't seen—or thought about—in all those years.

He wants to bust his brain—his balls, if must be—because his inner voice had called that vulnerable, nice woman's face a *mud duck melon.*

Someone taps in a strong rhythm on his shoulder.

As if it's a code.

Penman remains motionless, frozen in *the now.*

He does not dare to turn around, mortally afraid to face the Alien.

Brain Fever

*I*n the forties, it was chronicled that Father Ivo Guberina used to shout *Terra editus terrae redderis,* * [* bursting from the Earth, restored to the Earth] when, in cassock and with a machine-gun on his back, he tossed Serbian and Muslim women and children in the gorges of the Bivolje-mountains.

The Catholic priest performed this task in the name of God and His Holy Land Croatia, amen.

Guberina's *Ustashas*-brigade followed his example with gusto. They never tired of what he called "their patriotic duty."

In the choleric heat that envelopes London, I follow Father Guberina's grandson who's jogging in the well-to-do inner suburb of North Park. Tomas Mihic doesn't wear his grandfather's surname, but he's the grandson of the murderous priest alright.

That makes him a larva, a simile that Father Guberina liked to use to address people like my parents.

What do you do with creatures like that?

You crush them underneath your shoe.

***

Yoho, look at that: in spite of the heat, Tomas Mihic is celebrating a healthy Wednesday. He needs exercise, the pathetic fatty, he's panting like an overweight French bulldog, struggling to reach his house a few hundred yards farther down the road. His *house*? It's more like a mansion. The gaffer leads a copious life, working as a consultant for Racetrack LTD, a marketing agency specialized in political lobbying, and recently active in an expensive campaign to polish up Rwanda's image in the world-media.

A "new Rwanda," that's what president Kagame tries to evoke, and, having followed Mihic's work in the media for a few months, I must admit that the Rwandan president, aka mass-murderer, is on the right track to becoming *salonfähig*. Quite a talent, that half-nephew of mine.

No wonder that Tomas Mihic works for Kagame. His devoted Catholic grandfather was a mass-murderer too, preaching the Catholic Mass in Latin and doling out the Body of Christ, while leading the fascistic Croatian *Ustashas* during WWII in their bloody extermination raids against the Serbians and the Muslims. Father Guberina preached tirelessly from the pulpit, waving his arms like Moses parting the waters, his voice bellowing like God's trumpet. "The bodies of the Orthodox vermin and the Muslim-dogs cannot and may not be spared. Killing those doomed souls is an obligation to purge them of their sins. Cleansing our beloved motherland Croatia, the bastion of the Holy Catholic Faith, from these sinners is pleasing to The Lord. Afterwards, when their blood is spilled, come to me, and I will grant you Holy Absolution."

At times, while dawn creeps in my bedroom and buffets my dreaming mind, I have the distinct impression I can hear Guberina delivering his sermons, and before my mind's eye his black cassocked silhouette looms larger and larger until my heart is about to burst.

***

I'm pedalling leisurely and gaze at the mansions behind the rows of trees in North Park. No "new residential architecture" here, those *fata morgana* areas of London brimming with glass, concrete, and hardwood. North Park is much more blasé with its pompous imitations of the neo-classical villas of yore. Their owners try to imitate the nobility of the past, dreaming about being dukes and counts.

In the next instant, I am at Tomas Mihic's level. I go even slower and drink from my canteen. Out of the corners of my eyes, I peer at his swinging, wobbling body—absolutely a mini-whale, that one. Watch those bulky legs of my half-brother's son, hear him wheezing in the ozone-challenged air.

I pick up speed and cycle past him. When there is enough distance between us, I pretend there is something wrong with my bike. I step off and hold it by its front-wheel, facing his direction. I'm clad in the flashy attire of a fashionable cycle-tourist, helmet and sunglasses included. In this disguise, it's hard to see that I'm a seventy-two-year-old geezer. Tomas Mihic waggles my way, his arms dangling at his side. He resembles a giant penguin.

He passes me. I tell myself I can smell his fishy character. There is a drone in my torso, a breathless feeling. I glance at his back. I could have reached out and strangled him with all the strength that is left in my body.

But I'm not ready yet. I must bide my time.

When I kill him, I will make it look like the reason for the murder is something else.

There are so many possibilities. They confuse me. My head swims, drones, buzzes.

I could stage Mihic as an infidel, killed by the sword of Islam.

Or I could descend the wrath of the Christian God, The Father, on him, offing him with blows of a wooden cross, a weapon that his grandfather worshipped.

Maybe I'll use a crusader's sword, why not? That would be a nice touch.

I even know some Latin that goes with it. Or would that be too subtle?

Suo sibi gladio hunc iugulo. I forgot what it means, that's a shame.

Oh, such an overload of possibilities.

Makes me want to lie down and die.

***

I don't use the tube anymore. There are reasons enough for that but not one good.

In the bus, gazing out of the window, I see the districts becoming bleaker, the houses smaller, their facades smeared with soot. I feel that my resolution begins to waver. The Booming returns in full force in my ears. It does not tolerate any weakness in me.

I force myself to focus on the details of my reconnaissance of today, and reflect if I left any traces. I'm quite sure I did not. Someone who's got a crummy flat in Ferrers End, doesn't own a flashy bike. I've returned it to the cycle hire company, and paid a ridiculous fee. But it served its purpose, making me, together with my cyclist clothing, inconspicuous for the street cameras in North Park.

One day, in a not so far future, those cameras will be demolished by a raging army of people whom the government has let down again and again, pushing its arrogance in their faces. The mansions of the rich, and the rich themselves, will follow. I won't be around anymore when it happens. But before the light goes out, I must unload my own rage. Yet, although I'm feeling very determined, there are still moments in which I doubt if I'll be able to do it.

Focus/focus/focus.

Blandly gazing through the window at the neighborhood, I repeat countless times that it is my duty to revenge my mother.

She was a Muslim.

Dr. Ivo Guberina raped her.

I repeat, as many times, that my revenge is for my father.

He was a Muslim.

Guberina's *Ustasha*-thugs tortured and killed him.

Still, the question remains—will I have the guts to kill Guberina's grandson?

Is the son responsible for the sins of his grandfather?

How long has this mushroom of hatred and scorn in my head been growing?

Is it turning me into a lunatic?

It began with a whisper. After a while, it became a volcano in my head, ready to erupt.

Recently, it turned into the Booming.

In the lurching bus, I shudder in the same feverish way as I trembled fifty-seven years ago, at the moment in which I learned how my father died.

***

I was fifteen, when, in 1956, my uncle, who came frequently over to London from his home in Germany, desired that I should hear Ljuban Jednjak's testimony. Jednjak was the only Muslim who survived the *Ustashas*-slaughter in the village of Glina where I was born, and he was one of my father's friends. My uncle paid Jednjak a ticket to England. The old man didn't want to fly, came by train and boat instead.

A grizzled and dried-up Jednjak, gnarled as a centenarian tree, told me how, in May 1942, my father died by the hands of the oh-so-Catholic Croatian *Ustashas*-militia, led by one of the extremist Franciscan monks who were followers of the fascist Ivo Guberina. No one had ever talked about Guberina before. I was told that Guberina was a doctor of Theology. The doctor condoned the terrible bestialities of his horde of bloodthirsty priests, but also committed himself to give the example.

After his devout eruptions of blood thirst, doctor Guberina crossed himself, looked up at the skies, raised both hands, and prayed to The Father, the Son, and The Holy Ghost. After that, he absolved his pack and blessed them. They were patriots, performing a holy duty.

Although I was young, I realized why I had the feeling there was something opaque in Ljuban Jednjak's eyes. After all those years of re-membering what happened in Glina, there were no tears left in them. Jednjak had become a hollow man.

Thinking back at Jednjak, I realize that his testimony has galled me for decades, slowly scraping me empty.

So, now, each time I look in the mirror I see something opaque in my eyes.

My uncle recorded Jednjak's testimonial on his Revox tape record-er. I remember that I stared more at the machine than I was looking at Jednjak.

I still have his testimonial, re-mastered on a disk.

I play it almost daily, to confront the terrible pressure in my skull.

The resonance of the words strengthens the Booming.

***

We came from the fields, your father and I, and saw people running away in the distance. Women were crying. We hid ourselves in a deserted stable. Soon, through the meadows, we saw a long snake-like shadow moving. It was a row of men from the village, crawling on their belly through the field. They told us that armed Ustasha militia-men had raided Glina and deported all Serbs and Muslims from the age of fifteen on in a convoy of Lorries. The Ustashas told the villagers that they would have to follow a stringent religious training, and that those who converted to the Catholic faith would be allowed to return to their homes, while those who didn't would work in concentration camps.

We didn't believe a single word of it. We knew what had happened in other villages in the region. Your father didn't want to leave his wife and the baby—you were about a year old at that time—behind. I reasoned, even quarrelled, with him. Finally, he gave in. I'll never forget how he howled and clawed at his own face the moment he understood there was nothing that could be done to save his wife and child.

In a group of five, we fled through the woods toward the village of Belinac. Fate was against us that evening. At the entrance of the village, there stood a car with four Ustasha-soldiers. They arrested us and brought us to the church, pushed us on the floor, and searched our clothes for money. Your father, Ivica, resisted and was beaten savagely. They stomped him in the stomach, and between his legs. Ivica was a proud and resilient man. I pretended I was retarded and got away with some cuffs around the ears.

More than fifty men were locked up for two nights in the church without toilets, water, or food. On the third morning, the Ustashas came in the house of worship, and asked who of us knew Chetniks in the region. They said they wanted to teach those extremist Serbian pigs a lesson. Nobody answered. The beatings began, this time with the butt of their machineguns. At long last, they tired of this "small introduction to discipline." We had to swear that we believed in the Great Independent State of Croatia and the Revered Poglavnic* {* Ante Pavelic, leader of the Ustashas]. We shouted at the top of our voices that we truly believed, but they changed their mind, and said, "Wouldn't it be better for your depraved souls if we gave you the death penalty?" Ivica stood up. "Why would you kill us? We believe in the great Poglavnic, just like you." He lied, and the Ustashas knew it. They summoned him over. Two militia men took his arms, tied them together behind his back. Another took a candle from one the manifold holders spread everywhere in the church, and lighted it. He came and stood in front of your father, asked him, "So, you would follow our Poglavnic blindly, wouldn't you?" Before Ivica could answer, the Ustasha burned his left eye. Ivica's mustache also caught fire. It was horrible, the stench, the cries, your father's body trashing on the floor. It's an awful torture, the worst there is. They started burning his other eye. Almost simultaneously, two Ustashas beat your father with their rifle butts on his back and legs. Finally, they crushed his head with a sledgehammer. Pieces of his skull flew in the air. Some of them landed on me. A burst of machine guns followed. They were shooting at us, howling like wolfs.

I was hit in the shoulder and fell to the ground amidst dying and dead people. There came no end to the volleys. Then, suddenly, it was quiet; a high-pitched kind of silence as if the air was metallic and rang in a tone ladder we couldn't hear but still could feel. The Ustashas began to inspect the bodies. They sliced the throat of those who were not dead yet. They came nearer. A voice outside called them. They went out. I seized the opportunity to crawl under a dead man whose throat had been gorged. His blood ran over my face and neck. Some of it dripped in my mouth. The Ustashas came back, pushing Serbian prisoners toward the massacre. They had to take the bodies outside and load them in trucks. Three militia-men remained in the church. By the time it was my turn to be lifted off the ground, I was covered in blood. We passed the militia; I let my head loll. One of them looked at me, maybe only a second. It was like a vertiginous gorge in time. He turned his head again to his companions. I was tossed on a truck filled with bodies. A while later, the engine started. We were on our way. A little while later, I noticed that the truck turned right. I dared to lift my head slightly, and saw that we headed to Novo Selo. I knew there was a deep ravine not far from that village, and guessed we were going there. I was right. Ten minutes later, the truck stopped close to the edge of the gorge. Ustashas came over and began unloading the corpses. They took me by my arms and my head and tossed me over the rim. The corpses lying already in the ravine softened my fall, but I almost broke my neck when five or six more bodies landed upon me. Sometime later, I heard the militia driving away. I lay there for hours, knowing that other convoys would follow. Dawn came; no more trucks had delivered their load for more than an hour. I decided to run. My throbbing shoulder was stiff and painful, but I managed to leave the Clough by a rocky path that hunters had made years ago. In the village of Ukinac, kind souls rescued me, dressed my wounds, and fed me. I resolved to leave the country, and with a lot of luck, guided by Allah, I succeeded.

This is my story. It is your duty to remember it, and, if Allah is willing, to revenge the death of your dad.

***

I'm getting off the bus at Mafeking Road in a disturbed mood, and somehow exhausted. Traffic moving on the North Circular produces a constant droning. Three lanes in each direction, chock-full with nervous and aggressive chauffeurs. The results are lots of clumsy, horrible accidents, boozed drivers, sleeping drivers, mad drivers, and disrupted steel and shattered bodies. If we don't kill each other in war, our cars take over the job. The traffic used to be a reassuring sound in my younger years because there was a lot less of it. Now, it sounds like the rumble of advancing tanks.

I pass the Iraqi newsagent, who is standing in the doorway, as ever. People used to joke he was a spy for Iraq because he seemed glued to his doorway. I never saw anyone actually buying something in his shop. Next: a yellow dumpster overflowing with plastic debris, MC in black letters crudely painted on it. Clusters of Kurds live here. They're social, but sometimes newcomers ask me with taut faces if I'm Turkish. "No,"

I respond. "I'm not Turkish. I'm Croatian."

"You look like a Turk."

"We all look like Turks."

A row of cheap and battered cars line our street day and night. The only exception is the grey Porsche parked in front of number 213. It's not brand new, but definitely new enough to have been bought with drugs money. The owner, a bearded young guy, wears sunglasses, winter and summer. He tries to imitate what he would call a *nigger swagger*. Lately, he even wears a golden chain around his neck.

Thinking of the devil, there he is, carrying a big light-green bag over his shoulder. Deliberately, he stands in my way. Keeping my eyes on the pavement, I sidestep him. When I'm past him, he makes a sound like a noisy fart. Yeah yeah, I get the message, old fart, how original. I look up at the oversized TV aerial dish on the roof of his house, and muse about what I would do to him when I possessed a sword.

***

I ask my wife: "How was your day?"

Odela sits opposite me at the dinner table. She has prepared a *hallal* meal. quinoa, a salad with sunflower seeds, and lamb stew. She doesn't look me in the eye. Since a few months, she wears her scarf and *hijaab* also in the house.

She should see a psychiatrist. She really should.

"*Ed dounia mamzianache,*" she whispers.

I've heard her use that expression a lot lately. *The world is very bad today*. Odela is a peasant's daughter from the tiny village of Drakulici in Croatia. I learned about her via my mother's family, still living in Croatia. The marriage seemed a good arrangement. Now I know that I should have left her over there, instead of paying the dowry and the costs of her voyage to the UK. But in those days it was unthinkable to insult friends of your family like that. Moreover, I knew I didn't stand a chance with the English girls, those *tutholas*. Odela never liked England, but she was a good and obedient woman for a long time. Eight years ago, the woman she was vanished in some weird vacuum, a religious frenzy that I still cannot understand in spite of all my efforts. She talks more and more Arabic to me. She learns it in the Koran-school. Those throaty sounds get on my nerves. She reads the Koran five times per day, gently swaying her torso.

"I can't argue with that," I say. "The world is totally lousy today."

Odela is convinced it was written in some *soera* of the Koran that she would become disabled in the 7/7 bombing eight years ago. The cause of this verdict in the verses of the Holy Book? She hadn't been a good *Muslima*. She'd lived so long without her faith, she says, that something *had to* happen.

She used to sing a lot before the 7/7 bombing. She had a nice voice. Odela means melody in Croatian. Now, she limits herself to one tone of voice that irritates me, a sort of whisper that a frightened, but stubborn, child would use.

What can I say to her? My gaze wanders around our two-bedroom apartment on the first floor of a two-storey house, as weathered and sooty on the outside as most others on Mafeking Road, but renovated eleven years ago on the inside. We have spent years to make our flat cozy. We raided design stores, compared brochures. It was a nice pastime; we were a team. Look at the red curtains, the built-in flat-screen on the wall, the Swedish furniture that has cost us half-a-leg, the red Le Corbusier-chair, an almost perfect and pricy imitation.

Now, Odela disapproves of it all.

After thirty years of marriage, she also disapproves of me. When I drink a beer before the telly, I can feel how she loathes me. Her disapproving gaze surrounds me like a suffocating mist.

I don't want to ask her, but I do, as so many times before. "How, for fuck's sake, can you become a Muslima while *Muslims* have done this to you?" I point to her prosthesis, now invisible under her black *hijaab*.

Behold that holy light in her eyes. "My dear husband, you've become a *kafir* although your parents were of the Faith. You live with contradictions. They plague you, haunt you, and torture you. I left all of that misery behind the very moment I became a true follower of Allah. Allah set me free with His sublime and single truth. Everything is written. What happened to me was Fate. *Bismil'lah.*"

We continue our meal in silence.

"Josip, losing my leg was the best experience of my life," Odela continues minutes later, looking down at her plate. "It was the starting point for my journey to Allah, may His Name be blessed forever."

My Odela. My wife. She worked her whole life as a member of a cleaning crew in a hospital of the Croydon Health Services. She was fifty-six, when, on 7 July 2005, *jihad*-lunatics detonated their homemade bombs in the Underground and killed and maimed dozens of people.

Odela was among them.

It's beyond me to understand what she is becoming. Give her another year and she'll preach the *jihad* in the streets. Can you believe that? Can you fucking *comprehend?*

I stare at her, I do, I know. I also know there's a subdued panic in my eyes. I can see it mirrored in hers.

My wife, once such a dear partner, has become insane.

And part of me envies her.

At times, her insanity seems better than mine.

***

After dinner, she clears the plates. "Have you taken your pills?"

One mystery piled upon another. In spite of her aversion to my lifestyle, Odela still looks after me. Probably because Allah has ordained that a wife must be respectful to her husband.

After the pills, I stretch out on the sofa.

Although my parents were Muslims, I'm not. The belief that everything is predestined gives me the creeps, I guess because there has been so much powerless fury in my life. Was it predestined that I had to lose my mum and dad like that? Was it predestined that a shard of a self-made bomb cut off part of my wife's right leg in the 7/7 bombings? On that faithful day, Odela took, as usual, the tube at West Brompton station, while I drove the Circle and Metropolitan lines, sitting in the driver's cab of my train, looking ahead in the tunnels, going forty miles an hour, and seeing visions of my mother raped by dr. Guberina, of my father's eyes burning, of his scorched moustache, followed by a mirage that shows my train zigzagging like a giant snake and then crushing into the Underground-walls.

For so many years, I've been an Underground-driver with visions of death and torture on my tail. And when *real* death visited the Tube, I was miles away.

A crushing insecurity about *everything* has been present in my heart since I learned the facts about my parents. A month ago, it was replaced by a wild *exuberance* when, by chance, I read in *The Guardian* a report of *The Corporate Europe Observatory.* The piece was titled: *Spin Doctors to the Autocrats.*

And there it was: the name Tomas Mihic.

Barbir Mihic's only son, the article stated.

Barbir Mihic, my half-brother, born out of the raping lust of dr. Guberina, aka "The Iron Croate." After Guberina had raped my mother, he hit her with a heavy wooden crucifix on the head until he thought she was dead.

She wasn't. *Tanki** as she was, she was much stronger than she appeared. (*slender) Bloodied and exhausted, she picked me up at her parents, where she had left me the day before the *Ustashas* attacked our village. I was thirteen months old.

We both survived our escape from Croatia. On his turn, my half-brother survived in my mother's womb, although she tried to kill him more than once.

As soon as she gave birth to him in Germany, she deposited the offspring of her worst enemy in an orphanage in Munich. Two years later, my mother moved with me and my stepfather—a Brit who worked for an English company in Germany—to the UK. And later, much later, she attempted to trace that *other* child in Germany. Administrators went so far to reveal the name they had given the boy—Barbir Mihic— but she never found him.

I learned all that after my mother's death when I read her personal letters and diaries. She had never hinted at her past, didn't once mention the name dr. Guberina, nor told me that I had a half-brother and that she had searched for him when I was twelve.

But she had written it all down.

They are both long dead now, my mother Dafinka and her husband Steven Wrighton, who tried to be a true father to me.

My mum was a special woman who loved me dearly. She wanted me to become an engineer, but I was a wild and tempestuous teenager, probably because I had learned about my father's fate via my uncle, while my mum's obstinacy to keep her mouth shut about the past drove me to despair. Although I didn't have real recollections of papa, Jednjak's story and all the other tales of my uncle that painted the background of the mass-murders in Croatia during WWII, made me reckless and aggressive. In the end, I became a train driver. My mother was very disappointed.

I apologize for that now, ma.

You never complained or blamed me.

Sixteen years ago you died.

After the funeral, I opened your diaries and letters for the first time.

I learned who Barbir Mihic was. My half-brother, the cub of the man who raped you. That knowledge gradually poisoned me.

So here's the question, mother: did I find my half-brother's son *by coincidence*?

Was it, as they say, written by Allah?

Or guided by your spirit?

***

I don't have much time left.

I must act.

I remember the plans I've made since I first found out where Tomas Mihic lived, the revenge fantasies that gripped me.

In those daydreams, I break in Tomas Mihic's posh house, using some sophisticated movie-trick to disable the alarm-system. We fight, Michic and I, and, although much older, I use some sophisticated Chinese combat system to overpower him. I tie Mihic to a chair. His eyes bulge when he sees my *thobe* and the shawl draped over my nose and mouth. I don't have an explanation for why I see myself in classic Islamic clothing in those dreams. I read to Mihic parts of my mother's diaries. I play him Jednjak's disk. I unsheathe my sword; see the terror in his eyes, his propped-up mouth straining to yell.

His Adam's apple goes up and down.

Then, in a flash, the sword of vengeance cuts it in blood-spurting halves.

***

But reality isn't a fable in the middle of the night that kidnaps your mind, while you seem to be floating in a grey, immovable sea.

Can I do it? I ask myself in the darkness of our bedroom. Can I murder my half-brother's son to bestow my revenge on his bloodline? Barbir Mihic will never know I executed his son. He died of cancer ten years ago in Germany. I wish I had known about Tomas earlier, when I was less bitter and saner.

Why do I crave this revenge? In all likelihood, Barbir Mihic didn't know a thing about his past, and was not responsible for what happened to my parents.

Neither is his son Tomas.

The bloodline between him and me cannot be denied. Still, the thirst for requital is overwhelming.

My uncle told me many years ago that *Krvna Osveta*, the blood feud, was still practiced in his youth. He hinted that he had executed such a feud at the age of seventeen.

And thus became a man.

I'd love to hear his advice now, but his spirit doesn't reply to my questions.

Everyone has left me behind. I'm all alone.

Beside me in the bed, my wife snores.

She is a stranger to me.

And I to her.

Who am I?

Lately, I haven't the slightest idea.

A plan, a new plan, that's what I need. I must devise a workable plan.

With a clear voice, in her sleep, my wife says: "*El hassil, b'slemah, Josip.*

I know those Arabic words.

She is saying goodbye to me.

***

I'm trembling from head to toe. The handlebar of my hired bike shakes in my hands. I've taped the bike's brand name. Nothing more I could do to erase my traces.

My mind is an exploding fungus. It has sucked away all my sanity.

I wear my sunglasses, my bicycle helmet, my parrot-colored cycle clothing.

I pass him. He's a man of habits, Tomas Mihic. Very punctual, jogs every Wednesday from 3 p.m. until 4.

Look at him panting. His cheeks are bright red, almost the color of blood. He's grossly overweight.

That's very unhealthy.

***

I pass him. I don't give him a single look.

I'm brooding on something my uncle said, after he had played Jednjak's tape for the first time.

The eyes are the first to die; the nails the last.

What did he mean by that?

I'm nauseous. I'm dizzy. I don't feel well.

I cause my bike to welter. I Stop. Drop the bike.

I take a few faltering steps and grope for my heart-region.

I collapse to the grass, both hands clutching my breast.

Mihic is close now. I hear his breathing.

The knife is hidden in my left sleeve.

His shadow looms over me.

"Old man," Mihic pants. "Hey, old man, what's wrong?"

I stare at him through my sunglasses. He doesn't act like I hoped he would do. The prick keeps standing, instead of kneeling. He should kneel, the rapist's grandson. A gush of heat erupts inside me, as though someone has sprayed me with gasoline and set me on fire. I pull the knife out of my sleeve and plunge it in his left thigh. With a high-pitched wail, he clutches his leg and falls to the pavement like a marionette whose cords have been cut off.

I jump up, stoop over him, plunge the knife in his throat.

I hear a sound, a hoarse roar. It's me, yelling: "For my mother!"

I grab the bike. Jump on it. Peddle as hard as I can.

I'm looking straight ahead of me.

Deserted rich neighborhood, jolly good ha ha ha. All at the French Riviera, ha ha ha. Haven't seen a thing, ha ha ha.

What made me do it? I really just wanted to frighten him. After all the day-dreaming about impossible plots, there was no plan.

Or was there?

Is he dead?

Truly dead?

***

Daily Star—15 July 2013—page two

IRAN INVOLVED IN MURDER CONSULTANT?

Tomas Mihic, a consultant working for the contested marketing company Racetrack Ltd, which specializes in politic lobbying, was murdered yesterday, near his mansion in North Park. The murderer, clad in cyclist-attire and wearing dark glasses, cut Mr. Mihic's throat under the watchful eye of a security camera. Detective Chief Constable Paul Maroot of the Metropolitan Police Service declared that the images are being analyzed by a team of experts, and that "they will yield valuable information."

Racetrack Ltd refuses any comment, but our sources reveal that Mihic, born in the UK but of Croatian descent, was working on an "extremely sensitive" assignment. Unconfirmed rumors have it that Racetrack is planning a PR-campaign for Iran. The murder method seems to point to a typical Muslim execution. Again according to our sources, this hypothesis is very plausible: Iran, a major power in the Middle-East, is the arch-enemy of many Arabic countries.

An investigation into a homicide with a possible political background is always tricky, but Detective Chief Constable Maroot is convinced that the perpetrator will be arrested "with a minimum of delay."

Daily Mail—16 July 2013—page 21

SUICIDE DUE TO BRAIN TUMOR

On July 15, the 72-year-old retired tube driver Josip Kraci has committed suicide in his former work-surroundings. Apparently, Mr. Kraci used a service entrance to enter the tunnels of the Circle line. He lay down on the rails and waited for the train to arrive at 9.15 p.m. Mrs Kraci, his wife, confirmed the story that her husband Josip suffered from an untreatable brain tumor and said that his death was "Allah's will." Sources near to the investigation agree that all evidence points to suicide. Due to his cancer, Josip Kraci suffered intense pain and, according to a physician we consulted, "brain tumors of that type often cause "delusions, visions, and insanity."

Paint It Black

I

umultuous roaring. Very picturesque. Also very annoying. Peeping through the window. Peeping is an art form. Some houses farther, in the café at the corner of the *rue de Bosnie*, there is a top of the lungs argument. The curtains—red-and-white checkered—in the windows of café *El Principado* have been closed. I'm familiar with that sign: hoo-ha between Muslims and genuine *kiekenfretters*, as the residents of Brussels are nicknamed. Lots of creative curses and threats. Someone storms out of *El Principado*, chased by a heated individual armed with a wooden bat. Police sirens. Oh well, night business as usual in this working-class district of Brussels, the metropolis of *Manneken Pis* and the European Union, in that order.

I return to my atelier. I've equipped the veranda of the old house I'm renting with sunlamps, normally used for growing plants in winter greenhouses. The lamps are there to focus, to get the color right, to blindfold my dreams until they become paintings. Already, the title of my new painting has descended upon me: *Les mangeurs des enfants*. First I had *Cannibals*, but no, not intricate enough. *Les mangeurs des enfants* is disturbingly elegant. Politicians, clergymen, and teachers around the table, dissecting spastic young children. *Child Eaters*.

Spectacles on nose, brush in hand, anticipation in breast. What comes creeping? A void between the image I have of the picture, and the brush. The moment of magic is gone due to the argument at the café. Thank you, Brussels lowlife, thank you, followers of Allah. The ringing telephone is a God- given excuse to stop painting.

But who could be ringing at two o'clock in the morning?

***

"I noticed a pattern in your work, Drees De Grijse." Serge Butoyara talks with a drawl, not a good sign. "You can't paint a picture without at least one naked woman." Fuck, here we go for another nighttime telephone marathon. Serge is on the warpath again, fueled by God knows how many lagers, and wondering what is more important: his hatred for all living beings or his self-hate.

"It so happens that I love naked women, Serge."

A weird sound, something between chuckling and hissing. "So I noticed."

"Is that the reason for your call?" Something in me is stirring. It's caution.

"Each time I wanted to run away from home, my father threatened that he would cut off my big toe."

"Why your big toe?" Humor him, he'll get to the point. "Without your big toe you can no longer walk," Serge Butoyara clucks. "I already prepared myself for my new name: *Nak Gudwa.*"

"Oh?" Politeness is a wonderful thing. It makes you blank.

"It means *eight toes.* Why don't you come over and have a beer? Or we can drive to Paris and order champagne."

"Where is Jeanine, Serge?"

"Or we can fly to Stockholm. Picture it, Drees: a coal-black man like me in a pure-white world. Symbolic, don't you think?" Serge begins humming some lyrics of the Stones's "Paint It, Black." Nice falsetto.

"I'll come over one of these days and paint you in a snowy landscape, okay? Where is Jeanine?"

"She's on her knees right before you, Drees, and she has your dick in her mouth. You're swelling, oh yes, you're swelling, and she sucks slowly, only she knows how to do it like that—and you're laughing at me, you bastard, you think I'm a miserable joke."

Time to put down the phone.

Serge has figured it out.

What happened between me and his wife.

***

Three nights later. Telephone ringing. Picking up.

Sniffing sounds.

"Serge?"

No answer. Humming. Then: ancestral African dialects, who

knows what curse the damn Tutsi is reciting? I softly place the phone in its cradle.

Two minutes later: *ring ring*. Fuck off, Serge. But I know that I'll pick up again and be nice to him.

"Hello."

"A survival trip, Drees. The two of us. Now. A race to the finish. Parc de Forest…"

"And having my dick bitten off in the park by some mutts from those asshole dogfight organizers? I know better ways to get my kicks, Serge."

"I'm aware of that." He's being very polite. Not a good thing.

Silence. I'm a patient man.

"But you're out of touch as always," he goes on. "The cops have cleaned up the place. Bye, nightly dogfights… Only peaceful greenery now."

"I'm not a nature freak. Besides, it's well past midnight. I need my beauty sleep."

"A survival trip in the park as warriors. You and me. If we survive, we'll split Jeanine."

"Oh? Which part do you get?"

"Don't try to be funny, Drees. You're not. Never have been."

"Fuck you, Serge, it's one thirty. I want to sleep."

"Coward. No-balls-man."

"Okay, I'll be at your den within half an hour, you simian."

I know I shouldn't go. Serge is a wreck. He sniffs too much ether. I can't instill a more subtle need in him, like cocaine for instance. Ether in this day and age… How full of self-loathing can you be?

With Jeanine away on a trip to Italy, maybe I can convince Serge that it was her fault.

His wife seduced me, oh how she seduced me.

***

A confident push on the bell button. Drizzling rain in the middle of the night. A survival trip in a godforsaken Brussels park? Knowing Serge, it'll be a booze run again. Oh well, let's hope he has forgotten everything about Jeanine and me. He can't keep his thoughts together for longer than ten minutes; his short-term memory is fucked. That's why Serge is not a famous painter like me but a forger who earns lots of money, ten times the amount that I do, fucking celebrated as I am.

I don't have to worry. Serge won't hurt the man who sells his brilliant forgeries to Mafia men who in turn hawk them to rich nitwits.

But more than anything else: I don't want Serge to think that I'm afraid of him. The Tutsi thinks I'm a white shithead? I'll show him that Drees De Grijse is solid.

"Nagaibara, Drees!"

Oh Jesus, look at him standing in the doorway with his bells, his beads, a ring through his nose, his shield, his assegai. His long naked legs reflect the light of the street lanterns.

"And then they say I don't have all five together, you simian."

You should see his nostrils when he laughs royally, their delicate vibration.

In my car, I ask him, just to start some conversation: "Are you progressing with that forgery of the Greuze?"

That must be the source of his recent überfoolish behavior: the falsification of the Greuze is hellish work and demands tons of concentration and the lifestyle of a monk. Serge knows that. He must realize he's wasting time being mad because of Jeanine and me. When he's immersed in an all-demanding forgery, he knows that his wife has to freak out now and then. That's how Jeanine is; she has not been dealt with a generous amount of patience. She doesn't mean any serious harm.

"The Greuze is tougher than I thought, old chap." Now he sounds like some queer old Englishman. That means his condition is worse than I thought.

"Meijers is getting impatient."

"Meijers can drop dead and fuck his dead mother."

"Be careful with Meijers. He would follow your advice and then blow your brains out."

I'm the middleman between Meijers and Serge. Meijers makes tons of money on Serge's forgeries. For my part, I try not to complain.

Serge's mouth sags. He smells of gin. "I'm not careful. I'd rather die than be fucking careful."

"Okay, okay." I shouldn't pique him too much.

What I saw of the Greuze forging is perfect. In the Renaissance, Serge would have been a master painter. Now he's a falsifier who has to watch his step. The art business is controlled by gangsters. They're very civilized and all that, so they hire big guns when you're a pain in the ass.

Serge is always a pain in the ass, whether he's sober or drunk.

He once told me he killed his father when he was ten. I don't buy it. He has a big mouth and lots of delusions. It's been a few days since he told me he knew about Jeanine and me, and everyone is still alive.

So why should I be afraid?

***

While I park the car on *l'avenue du Parc,* Serge mumbles: "What would you do if you thought you had cancer?"

"Spend all my money on one gigantic party with naked black women in, yeah, spatterdashes, their bellies circled by beads in the most politically incorrect colors. We'd bathe in champagne and perform exquisite and lavish hanky-panky, then take the plane to Gauguin's grave where I would put a bullet in my head while my Negro goddesses chant some heavy gospel."

"I think I have cancer." Serge points at his crotch. "There. Ball cancer."

"In civilized countries they have ball doctors."

The whites of his eyes suddenly seem extremely bright in the light of the street lanterns that bestow a romantic touch upon *Parc de Forest.* In daytime, lovers walk the park lanes holding hands. People who hold hands can save the universe. Serge and I don't hold hands.

"Serge Butoyara in a hospital?" he says. "A warrior in a sickbed that you can adjust to sixteen positions?"

"Don't you think you exaggerate a little with that warrior pose?"

"I'm not exaggerating enough."

"Cancer, my ass. I bet it's just a nervous breakdown of your niggerish thingy due to stress."

"Oh? And how, pray, has my niggerish thingy become so nervous, Drees, my dear friend?"

"How should I know?"

Serge doesn't answer and stares past me at the trees, the strategically placed small sculptures in the park, the romantics, and so on. I've always considered trees to be sneaky bastards and at night they're even worse. Greenery is for animals. I like street scenes filled with Flemish lowlife and the smell of paint.

When he gets out of the car, Serge's plumage hooks behind the door.

"Did you think you're Shaka Zulu? And where did you get those feathers?"

"From the Senegalese Dance Theatre. They performed in Brussels yesterday. At the Ancienne Belgique. I told them I was looking for props for a painting."

"Wait a second."

I take a picture of him.

In black-and-white.

***

My lungs are about to burst. I try to keep my eyes steady on the feathers before me. I may be almost forty-nine but I have the heart of a thirteen-year-old, give or take a few years. Serge doesn't do a freaking thing all day except paint, munch fast food, and gulp down weird cocktails of his own making. But now it seems he has grown wings. His long, sinewy legs pump up and down with terrible efficiency.

"Serge! There! A rabbit! Spike it with your assegai!" My voice is croaking. Serge doesn't stop, doesn't even turn his head. I'm wheezing like an old cow. I get it: he wants to humiliate me. I have to come up with another trick to hide the fact that he's much younger than I am and that his breath takes him much farther than mine. I'll pretend that I'm tripping over something and—

I trip over a tree root; pain shoots through my left ankle. I cry out, with my nose engulfed in the rich smell of dung and leaves. I roll over and grasp my ankle with both hands. The pain fades slowly. I groan loudly again just to be sure that Serge gets the message. Yeah, I'm having a ball lying on the wet ground in the fine drizzle that sweeps over a very somber Parc de Forest at two thirty a.m. Loneliness, that's what I feel. Even the street lanterns of avenue de Forest behind that wall of trees seem a galaxy away.

Serge has stopped running but doesn't inspect my injury. The way he's standing, he is really looking down on me. His naked chest gleams as if it's oiled.

"Don't shine your flashlight in my eyes, damnit… Help me!"

Serge doesn't move a finger. The light from a street lantern some ten meters away polishes his assegai with an eerie glow.

"It's because of Jeanine, Drees, that I'm feeling this way."

"This way? What way?"

No answer. Suddenly, I'm not feeling so secure. Why didn't I turn my heels and go home the moment I saw him standing in full African regalia in his doorway?

"Don't start again, Serge. Better help me."

"I know how Jeanine is. When she closes the door of our house behind her, she is not the same as when she's with me. I understand that. I've learned that. If she has some booze in her delicious belly, she becomes another person. Eight times out of ten she comes back to our house unblemished, where I sit and wait. Maybe even nine times out of ten…"

"Serge, I think my ankle is broken. And don't be so melodramatic! Shaka Zulu gets paid to rant like a biblical prophet on TV."

"Those other times, those few other times, those very few other times… well, I don't know. Maybe there have been other such occasions. I don't want to know about them. They don't understand Jeanine, they don't know me. But you… you know both of us. And I am a very old-fashioned man: I value my honor."

I try to get up. I can handle this. I must be able to look him straight in the eye.

In spite of the biting pain, I crouch up on one knee. Softly, Serge pushes me back with the shaft of his spear.

I remember clearly how excited I was when Jeanine finally gave in a month ago. Probably she was weary of my endless cajoling. Or maybe I had made her curious bragging about my prowess in bed. Jeanine turned out to be far from a disappointment. I flew on cloud nine when I left her in the drab hotel room we had rented to make it more sleazy. I was mighty flattered. But later that evening, I began worrying about Serge. Suddenly I strutted a lot less. This simpleton, this gifted artist, this goddamn Tutsi, was my friend. A friend who loved his wife definitively and was very possessive of her. Oh Jesus, I thought, no good can come from this. I telephoned Jeanine, told her precisely that. A hoarse chuckle, followed by a whisper: "It wasn't worth it." I didn't ask what Jeanine meant by that and hung up.

"Surely your honor can wait till we get home—we're not in some kind of backward bush here. We're in Belgium, for God's sake."

"You could have asked me for money. I would've given you money to visit the most exquisite Somalian hooker in Brussels. Your hairy white body pressing against a woman the color of old copper, with muscles like an antelope—wouldn't that have been a sight to behold?" He pushes the assegai against my belly button. "Hmm?"

"Oh yeah, a treat, definitely. You can't blame Jeanine, Serge. I was like a cockroach to her, blinded by the light... It was stronger than myself." I try to push the spear away. "Actually, I didn't really want it to happen." The spear doesn't yield a millimeter.

"But still you made it happen."

"Because Jeanine is the snake in paradise, you fool! You of all people should know that!"

"Narobong geteng ino." The spear is traveling down my belly to my balls.

"Oh God, not this mumbo-jumbo again. This is not the moment for silly curses, Serge."

"The correct translation is: *Go fuck an ox.* I can even transform you into one."

"In that case, I prefer you slicing my throat, if you don't mind."

Fast as lightning Serge plants the spear between my legs, only a breath away from my testicles, into the ground. Ay, oh my, I can see raw passions marching over his face.

"I was just a fancy for her, Serge, but only you can truly handle her, you're the man... If only you could see that."

"That's not what this is all about."

"It's exactly what this is all about."

I struggle upright, lean against a beech tree. A flash of brown and silver. With great power the assegai is pushed into the tree, again with uncanny precision and this time only a whisper away from my head.

We eyeball each other.

"You're not going to off me, are you, Serge?" I try to stretch my leg, but the pain in my foot makes me somersault down on my ass again.

"You're under my spell now, fish belly. You'll never touch a woman again, and you can forget painting anything meaningful from now on."

"Never again?"

"Never again, Mr. Pale Dick."

"Okay. I'll never touch a woman again, and from now on I'm a lousy painter."

"You remain my best friend. But from now on you'll be a lousy painter."

We exchange crooked smiles.

Then Serge lifts me off the ground and carries me to the car. He decides to drive when it becomes clear that I can't use the clutch with my right foot.

The whole way back I'm sweating blood and water. At this hour there are almost no living souls on the road, but Serge has only once before in his life driven a car: when he let his white Belgian father bleed to death in the bush.

***

"Drees, light of my eyes! I'm in the Hilton bar. Meet me here, we have to talk."

"I'm very busy, Eliath."

"Oh, painting a masterpiece again? Why should you? So famous already! Must be no fun being workaholic Drees De Grijse. Come on, let's wine and dine at *Comme Chez Soi.*"

"I'm having it here, *comme chez moi*, Eliath."

"Drees, be nice to me. I want to talk about Serge. That boy's in great trouble. He's a bigger hassle than the whole goddamn intifada. I'll have to set him straight, teach him the ropes."

"I'm on my way."

Cursing the whole way in the car. Traffic jam in the city center. I crawl toward the boulevard *Emile Jacqmain* and the Hilton at the *Place Rogier.* Oh well, the painting I was working on when that bastard Meijers called has every chance of becoming a failure anyway. *Les mangeurs des enfants* is eating me.

In the Hilton bar, I only have to follow the din to find Eliath Meijers. With great cunning, he wears the disguise of a potbellied sugar daddy. In reality, he nearly chokes on his own venom. Meijers is the CEO of an import/export firm and has Lebanese—a Lebanese pretending to be a Jew—and Belgian citizenship, is registered in Liechtenstein but lives in the well- to-do village of Drogenbos near Brussels. He is married to a Dutch *Valkyrie* by the name of Birgit Waarsenbergs.

Underneath the mask of the jolly uncle who's fond of tasteless jokes, Meijers is the uncrowned king of the murky trade in very expensive and very fake paintings.

"Sit down, Drees." Blinking innocently at me, he taps the stool next to his well-filled ass.

I sit down close to him and put my right arm around his shoulder, pushing my thigh against his. "Come on, Meijers, don't be shy, give me a tongue dance."

Grinning, he leans over so I can kiss his Azzaro-sprinkled cheek. He would like to cuddle me, I'm sure, but we're not alone. Off to the side, one of his bodyguards is staring through his glass of tea at us. His face is consumed by the solipsism of Allah's righteousness.

Meijers glances at me, his eyes flickering mischief. "You've become fat."

"What, you don't have a mirror at home, Meijers?"

He has watched too many classic mob movies, ingested too much Hollywood. He wants to be treated like a capo and I'm treating him like he's Dostoevsky's Idiot.

"A drink? Some food? They have delicious—"

"No, I don't want a drink or some food. Let me guess why you wanted to see me: you've decided you have way too much money and you want to bestow it on me as redemption for your many bloody sins."

He chuckles, but not too enthusiastically. There is something on his mind.

"If you want me to falsify a Mondrian for one of those über-rich, stiff-upper-lip bitches who can't see the difference between a toddler's drawing and an algebra exercise, then the answer is no."

Meijers pretends he's laughing so hard that he's nearly suffocating in his next gulp of coffee. He simply loves my charade and so he acts as if I'm his idol.

"You're still boxing, *garçon*? Oh, you've got those heavy, strong arms. Let me pinch them, come on, they can't be real."

"No English boxing, Meijers. Nippon kempo and Thai box."

"Could you beat a regular, sound boxer with all that fancy Eastern stuff, Drees? Can you prove it to old Meijers? I'll arrange something. No-holds-barred."

"That sounds to me like an old-fashioned street fight, Meijers. Good enough for me. But I'll bring my own assistant. Yours would drug my drink so that you could win the bets you'd surely organize."

Roaring laughter. Eyes toward the ceiling, exposing his throat.

We look each other in the eye. We're akin. We're not friends.

"Serge has threatened me." Meijers always changes the subject like that. And never, ever, even during the most delicate conversations, does he lower his voice. "He said he would show me the color of my intestines with his assegai, something like that, very poetic, that boy. Such a beautiful kid, totally different from you, Drees, you hairy ape… Serge is a… a reed, a gleaming black stallion, a—"

"Let me guess: Serge threatened you because you paid him a lot less than what you'd promised for the false Greuze."

Meijers leans toward me. Tiny beads of sweat on those bulldog cheeks. I don't like the man but he's never stood in my way. He loves money. I love money.

"You know him well, Drees. You think he's up to it? You should've seen him foaming at the corners of his mouth. A creature of the wild from top to bottom."

Before my mind's eye, with razor-sharp precision, I picture Serge in the Parc de Forest, his assegai pointed toward my balls.

No, Serge isn't up to it. I chuckle.

"Why the laughing?"

"He slaughtered his own father, Eliath."

His small eyes blink into mine.

"Serge is as mad as an armadillo with tropical fever rattling in his skull." I'm on a roll now, puffing steam. Oh hell, this is exhilarating. "I would be very careful if I were you. And afraid."

"Did he really kill his own father?"

"He told me the story, every detail of it."

"And you believe him?"

"Fucking A."

Eliath sighs, slurps the last drops of his coffee. He groans like a small child plagued by a nightmare.

"He has a pretty wife, Drees. And what I heard is that you—"

"Gossip. People project their dreams onto me, Eliath. Why? Because I am the Artist with a capital fucking A. I rob their souls and transcend—"

"Yeah, yeah. But Serge..."

"Oh, he'll get you sooner or later. The things he'll do with your puny circumcised dick, sweet Lord, I don't even want to think about..."

"Drees, you foul-mouthed barbarian, I'm so fond of your blabber." Meijers smiles. His eyes reflect the light, nothing else.

"How's your daughter doing?" If he can change subjects abruptly, so can I.

Gitte, Meijer's daughter, is a bouncy, black-haired teenager with Lolita eyes. She leads Meijers by the ring in his nose. Nasty rumors suggest that Gitte can't be his—the beauty and the beast, etc. Whatever. If you want to change the subject, just mention her name and he goes off like a firecracker.

"She's the light of my life, Drees. She's so *artistique*. Of course she must grow. She adores your paintings and she thinks you're real macho. But tell me more about Serge."

Ooh la la, so quickly with his feet on the ground again: Serge is for sure weighing heavy on his mind. Let's rev it up here…

Half an hour later I say goodbye. As a bonus, on top of the bloodcurdling stories I invented about Serge, I lick Meijers, grunting like a Labrador, over his mustache while bear-hugging him. His upper lip tastes of sour sweat and pomade.

The whole trip back to my house, although stuck for a long time in a traffic jam again, I'm grinning like a lunatic.

***

Three weeks later, someone—I don't recall his name, which is strange, it must have been a mutual friend and I don't do ether—told me that Serge's body had been found in a crack in a rock in the vicinity of the village of Beez, close to Namur, in the Ardennes. Suicide by hanging was the verdict.

Jeanine looked gorgeous at Serge's funeral, graced by the attendance of nearly the whole Tutsi clan of Brussels. A journalist and art critic, whose blood I could drink, told me a few days ago that rumor has it that a doctor sedated Jeanine so she could attend the funeral. According to him—frog's eyes and a Schiller collar—the drug made Jeanine look even more torpid and defenseless than usual, and thus even sexier. He also wanted to communicate that Serge had squandered his huge talent—but I cut him short: "Serge Butoyara was a much better painter than I could ever be." I saw in his face that I had sold him a headline for his next article.

Eliath Meijers didn't attend the funeral but he did send an enormous garland, flashy as a parrot. The monstrous thing had to be carried by three men.

Listen carefully: I am 100 percent sure that it was suicide. Meijers had nothing to do with it.

Serge was that unstable type you find everywhere: unable to give his life shape and meaning.

If we painters can't give shape and meaning to mankind's measly existence, who can?

Moreover, not everything I told Meijers was a lie.

Serge really killed his father.
He confessed it to me.
A story like a nightmare, really.

***

"We were cruising through the jungle, Drees, my father and I. He was a freckled Flemish redhead. Imagine that. I never knew how he survived Rwanda's mighty sun. Freckles... in our sunbathing mountains.

"He used to beat my mother and me. We lived in Save, at his mission post in the mountains. Yeah, sure, Rwanda is the African equivalent of Switzerland and all that crap...

"I never knew what he was thinking or what kind of mood he was in. He hardly spoke to me, except when he hit me. On those occasions, he grunted the same expression over and over again, a Flemish curse I suppose. Oh, almost forgot: each morning he would snarl the day's chores at me. So much for conversation between father and son.

"I used to look at his reddish fringe of beard that kept rising and falling like a small ferocious animal when he was cursing at my mother and me.

"We rode into the valley of Save, had to stock up on supplies. My father drove the Land Rover hard, as usual. I don't remember much about the accident. At the moment of the crash, I was staring at the sky going misty behind the ridges and fantasizing about the mythical Rwandese hero Ryangombe, who my mother used to tell me stories about. That very morning she'd related the tale of how Ryangombe threw himself on the horns of a giant bull to save other people. I was wondering why Ryangombe had done such an utterly foolish thing. He had to know that he would be punctured, the moron. The tip of the Nubaru Mountain suddenly tilted. Something seemed to puncture me and I heard a thrilling cry, like that from a bird of prey, precisely the same cry that Ryangombe had uttered when he died.

"When I regained consciousness, the Land Rover was lying on its side next to me. My father's upper body stuck out of the window. My back hurt, but I seemed okay. I stumbled toward my father. Blood trickled down into his red beard, pooled upon his closely shaven skull. His eyes, however, were open.

"*Open the door, boy, help me.* So soft, his voice. I had never heard it before, that kind of tone. It scared me. As if a ghost in his head was talking to me after he had left his body.

"Now he looked at me. What he saw made him turn his eyes away.

"What I saw made me turn *my* eyes away.

"I sat down beside him and I watched the mist engulfing the faraway ridges, like bleached cotton on black river pebbles. The village of Save was close enough to go there by foot and ask for help. My father didn't mention the car door anymore. He remained silent. When I stole a glance at him, he was staring at a pebble on the ground.

"I stayed sitting there until dusk. I must have been there for about nine hours, but I didn't feel hungry or thirsty. When three farmers found us, there was no breath left in my father's breast.

"The farmers couldn't drive. I told them I could. Between the four of us we managed to get the car upright.

"We drove back to Save. I was immensely proud behind the steering wheel with the three farmers crowded together in the front seat and the body of my father bouncing up and down in the back. Faster and faster we went. It was the ride of my life. When we arrived, the farmers, myself, and my father's body were covered with gray dust.

"The farmers said I was crazy. I had driven so fast I could hear the wind whistling in my hair.

"And I told them that from now on, my name was Serge Butoyara, my mother's name."

***

You dream of me while I'm crouching on your chest like the simian you said I was, Drees.

Shed my leading role in your nightmare. Wake up and move that bleached old man's body.

Don't lie snoring contently in your bed with your mouth wide open.

Your closed eyes don't fool me.

You're awake and still you can feel me, can't you?

You have killed me just as I killed my father.

Get up.

Don't you hear the telephone ringing?

You've had many calls over these last few days.

Breathing calls.

Your phone is ringing in the middle of the night.
Any moment now, you'll open your eyes, you'll bolt upright, grab the phone.
You'll hear the breathing.
Maybe Meijers has decided that you've become a liability.
That you know too much about Serge and him.
Maybe a woman whose heart and soul you wounded is planning revenge on you.
There... there you go, Drees...
Only the sound of breathing and the thumping of your heart.

II

You want to understand my artistic vision of life?

Okay, take a peek at my last painting. Took me months, an Eiffel Tower of Campari bottles—yes, I drink Campari, dick-head—and buckets of sweat.

After that canvas, I haven't had a single brush in my hand.

And I finished it a year ago, go figure.

I'm sure Serge managed to implant the horrid image in this fine piece of art in my brain. *From now on you'll be a lousy painter.*

Revenge from the grave.

I exhibited the painting in the Memorias gallery in *de Wolstraat*. It was a group exhibition, so I thought I could risk it.

"Has the Renowned Artist Drees de Grijse Gone Mad?" was one of the headlines of a critique in a "quality newspaper."

For sure drunk and stoned and deep in Alzheimer's, that slimeball.

My artistic thesis for this painting is as follows: life is one of those giant eels crawling in a muddy seabed with a maw bigger than its tail.

So I went ahead and painted one of these fuckers. What's the big deal? Pic-fucking-asso would've gotten away with it.

Okay, my background—nothing but mud and slime—is a bit monotonous on the canvas.

But the eel... man! The eel's head looks more like a suction cleaner, actually. Sucks everything into the shit deep under the muddy water.

When life wiggles its tail, you hope something out of the ordinary will happen; you fall in love, you betray your best friend, you fuck his wife, you endure painter's block.

You do those things and the result is a shitload of problems. Your best friend ends up dead, followed by night-calls—*pant pant, wheeze wheeze*—mystery, suspicion, fear.

And a thumping heart.

And then—nothing.

No more calls. No more mystery. People do normal things again. The woman named Jeanine, a dangerous sphinx in my opinion, moved to Amsterdam to become the lover of the proprietor of a goddamn weed shop.

As if that woman isn't already high enough from herself.

So you forget what happened. So easy to settle again, squander your days, waiting for your earthly demise—in the meantime wining, dining, fornicating.

But not painting. The famous Drees de Grijse has retired, hey-ho.

Only, just when I—by pure luck—had sold my exceedingly *mauvais* eel painting to one of those blasé MEPs wasting the European taxpayer's money—he considers my eel avant-garde!—precisely then, life immediately grabs my throat again.

***

Brussels may be an unkempt and filthy city with way too much traffic coursing through it, and with an architecture that has no spirit to offer except greed and contempt, but the pearl-gray light of a September evening can turn some of its corners into a cozy fantasy.

I'm sitting on the terrace of *Marché aux puces* on place *Jeu de Balle* with a half-empty bottle of Campari, celebrating the sale of my horror painting, simultaneously wrestling, however, with a linguistic problem. There was a time when *puces* meant *hookers,* wasn't there? Or does it only mean *flies?* The Campari and the candy colors of some of the nineteenth-century houses surrounding the plaza, bordered with sycamores, don't do much to enlighten me. Hookers—definitely.

"Drees! Drees de Grijse! Of all people... Coincidence doesn't exist."

I look up.

What a coincidence.

Gitte Meijers. Little Gitte. Daughter of Eliath Meijers and Birgit Waarsenbergs. The light of Eliath's eyes. And he had such tiny piglet peepers, the scumbag.

Gitte Meijers. Her eyebrows so wide, her upper eyelids painted black, her face geisha-white, her lips dark as sea anemones, stars on her cheeks, tattooed *mandalas* on her arms.

She's—what—eighteen, nineteen now? In spite of her extravagant makeup, she has that dark look of her father. How long ago kaput, that hog Meijers? Two, three years? Time flies and all that jazz. Some devilish cancer. Pancreas? In any case, it went lightning-fast. Great reception after the funeral. Lots of expensive booze. Blond Birgit looked extremely fuckable in her black outfit. I told her so and she agreed.

Her daughter wears a bodysuit with fucking beach sandals, the outfit a maze of white and gray circles. She moves *en vogue*, yeah.

"Do you like my color palette, Drees?" She points to her face.

"*Bellissima.*"

"Going to a dance party." She comes closer, almost leans over my shoulder. "Did you know that I have reproductions of all your paintings in my room?"

"Kneel before them every evening and say your prayers; they'll bring you luck."

She laughs. She's young; she doesn't sense that I'm tense. Gitte. Gitte Meijers.

"Want to come along? I was waiting for my friend, but he's more than an hour late." A shrug of her slender shoulders. "These days he's more obsessed with dealing than with me." Her face brightens. "There will be a top-class deejay at the rave."

With some decorum, I grope in my leather jacket and put on my dark glasses. She giggles. Years ago, I wrote a threatening letter to her father, stating that I knew he was a murderer. I didn't send it. Instead I buried the letter in the small village of Beez, close to Namur, in the Ardennes. In a certain crack in a rock. There, I asked Serge's spiteful spirit to take revenge on Meijers, sooner or later. I was apeshit drunk, so I forgot my vow; however, nature in the form of Meijers's cancerous pancreas did the rest.

Much obliged, nature.

***

Hours later. Gitte isn't going to no party. She sits on the terrace with me, listening breathlessly to my ramblings about one of my forefathers who was of Spanish descent, and a nobleman to boot. Sadly enough, that *capitano* couldn't resist raping girls. "*Querida, querida!*" he howled during his vile acts, whereupon, his beastly lust quenched, he strangled those poor lasses.

She giggles. The filly giggles.

I'm wearing my leather jacket, my floppy hat, and my dark glasses. A little chill in the September air; I see her sitting hunched over. When will she grow tired of the bullshit I'm feeding her? I resort to silence.

She clears her throat. "Drees, you know… I'm also into painting. I would be very flattered if you would…"

Oh God. So that explains her patience with my oafish tales. Look at that: poignant hesitation, fluttering eyes, the works. "Would you care to see them and give me some pointers?"

"Where's your studio?"

"I don't have a studio yet… but I paint every day!"

Every day. Christ Jesus.

***

She owns an MG. Fiery red.

"Did you drink much?"

"Only a Campari or two." Let's see how observant she is. The bottle stood between us on the table. Empty.

"Care to drive?"

"My pleasure."

When I'm drunk, I remain lucid. I take risks though. They make my tummy tingle.

I'm fucking Stirling Moss, that's who I am. Gitte shrieks in delight in the MG's small, leather-clad cabin while I skid along the road. Her pert butt quivers along with the hard suspension of the small sports car.

"I got stuff in my apartment. Want some?"

Hadn't expected anything else.

"*Dux femina facti.*"

"What did you say?" She puts her left hand on my knee. Just a tiny moment, but the hand was there.

"Latin wisdom. Look it up. What kind of stuff you got?"

"Cocaine. Gift from my boyfriend. Market's best."

I push down on the accelerator.

***

Her student apartment in a stately nineteenth-century town house, built in French neo-Renaissance style, on *rue des Moines*, is a bit petit bourgeois, in spite of the old radio casing, now serving as a planter, and the oversized xylophone in a corner. In another: a balloon with a lipstick heart on it, tied to a broom.

"Conceptual art?"

She shrugs and then rummages through a drawer of the fairly unclean small kitchen. "Just a joke. It was meant for my boyfriend, but he left it here."

"Being disrespected is manna for the artist's soul."

She looks up swiftly, as if frightened by something. That curtain of coal-black hair reminds me of Eliath.

"Where are your paintings?"

"Later. I don't have them here."

"I thought that Eliath's daughter would be housed in a place a bit more luxurious."

This time she doesn't look up. "My mother owns the house and rents the other apartments. I wanted to live here."

"Between the riffraff."

Smiling. "Yes, between the riffraff."

"What are you looking for?"

"Attributes." What a strange word for that kind of girl.

In the farthest corner, there is a small bookcase.

Metamorphoses Book 2.

"You read that?"

"Hmm?"

"You read Ovid?"

"Why not? My father loved him."

Jesus, the pitiless Eliath Meijers was fond of Ovid. So it's true: mankind is inscrutability incarnated.

She reappears in the living room with an old-fashioned snuffbox. "It's about changes."

"So I gathered."

"I would like to change."

"Change isn't like putting on another dress."

She opens the box and lays out two generous lines on the coffee table. "You believe in life after death?" she asks, seemingly nonchalant.

I must cut this shit off, snort my free line, and get the hell out of here.

"You believe in life before death?"

That look again, as if frightened by something. She doesn't answer, bows her head to the first line. Her mascara is a bit smeared, as if she was crying in the kitchen. I follow her example, our heads nearly touching above the small table.

"Oh, wow... Gitte, I'm on fire. I see your father burn in hell. I stand next to Eliath and, man, he's burning real good."

She offers me a smile that should be knowing and conquest-minded, but fails miserably.

***

I've heard my own voice telling her everything about Serge and my suspicion that her father killed the raving Tutsi. Gitte rolls her eyes. Red-cheeked and huge pupils—this baby chick is getting off on her father's sins, if you ask me. Her head pulsates. Oh wow, am I really that high? Like a Boeing 727?

"Interesting." She yawns. "But I liked your *capitano* story better."

"Oh?"

"*Querida! Querida!*" she crows.

I get the message.

"Where are your paintings?"

"In my mother's house."

"She still lives in that mansion in Drogenbos?"

"Yeah."

Silence.

"So, let's go."

"Now? It's half past one."

"Art knows no time."

"Maman will be asleep."

I get up. I want to know if the daughter of Eliath Meijers has it in her. "No problem. She'll be glad to see me."

"Did you date her after my father died?"

"Of course I did. And we called it *fucking.* Come on, let's go."

She rises slowly. Suddenly, I pity her and that makes me even more vicious.

"Hurry up, your friends' panties will get wet when you tell them what fun you had with the notorious Drees de Grijse."

She shakes her head, a bit compassionately, it seems. "They only get wet for pop stars."

***

We're at the door when she says: "Just a minute." Leaving me standing by the front door, disappearing into the kitchen again. Coming out with another snuffbox, this time a blazing red one with a bright yellow star on it. "Before we go, a special treat. It isn't every day that a humble young woman like me receives a visit from the great Drees de Grijse."

Is that irony? Derision, even? Payback for my remark about her mother?

Her eyes are bright and shiny. "A special blend, concocted by my friend. Real designer stuff." She beckons me over to the coffee table.

A minute later I'm snorting like a delighted horse.

When we descend the stairs, it dawns on me that she hasn't tried the designer stuff herself.

***

It's warm in the MG's cabin. Outside, a capricious wind blows.

She drives fast and recklessly.

"I haven't painted in over a year now," I say.

She doesn't react.

"I've filled 168 canvasses. I'm fifty. Why should I go on?"

"Because you can't do anything else."

She hunts the night with her red car and I ponder what she said. It can't be that simple, can it?

At our right skulks the Anderlecht Canal. She takes the rue de Biestebroeck, speeds toward the Quai de Biestebroeck.

Maybe she has a mind as deep as the canal, maybe she's... What's this? I have the sudden feeling—the certitude—that Serge is coming for me with a vengeance..

I start to sweat. Is my head lolling on my neck? Am I losing control over my muscles?

Do I hear her laugh softly?

What has she given me?

I see it. The Land Rover. At the opposite side of the quay. No lights on. A dark vehicle of doom. It's charging toward us. The flaming ghost of Serge Butoyara at the wheel, and I know he can't drive.

Look at Serge laughing; this ghost of flames and fury is having wicked fun.

I grab the MG's steering wheel and turn it sharply to the right. The lightweight sports car veers off the road, crashes against one of the iron poles lining the *quai of Biestebroeck*, and screeches when it starts spinning like a carnival ride.

Then there is the feeling of zero gravity.

A deafening splash.

A spine-jolting shock.

***

Double vision.

It's worse. Double *me*.

I'm floating above the canal; I see white moonlight bobbing on the water.

I'm also in the sinking car. Getting very dark in here. What a breathtaking sight, this fluid darkness. The girl beside me screaming, her head bloody against the steering wheel. Water gushes through the leather canopy of the convertible. My other me, floating like an angel above the water, signals that I must turn down the window. I obey. The canal water stinks. The door opens. Where is Gitte? Too dark to see.

I feel a jolt like an electric current when I'm reunited as one.

I'm a strong man, a good swimmer. My head surfaces—and who is fluttering above? Goddamn Serge. His smile is as cold as the whole fucking North Pole and South Pole combined. I cough. The high cranes at the other side of the canal resemble the martians in that black-and-white movie of the H.G. Wells story. Cold, it's so cold in the water. I swim toward the gently sloping shore where the concrete quay ends. Ever so slow. But fucking Serge is screaming that I will live, that I have to suffer some more before I perish. That godforsaken black ghost hits the nail on the head. Where's the fucker now? Vanished already, like always when the going gets tough.

Feeling mud under my feet. Stagger up the slope. Wind tugging at my wet clothes.

Turning around. Facing the dark water, the martians, the pale concrete quay.

"Gitte!"

No Gitte rising out of the waves. No floating head that I can rescue and kiss passionately.

Only wind and waves.

And my brains bursting apart, suffering the power of one hell of a designer drug.

***

I'm in survival mode.

Yeah.

I'm only body.

The body thinks: *Dry clothes, warmth, house, shelter.*

The body thinks: *Nobody will know that Gitte Meijers had a passenger. The water will have cleaned my presence from the car.*

The body has instinct.

The body feels wallet in leather jacket.

It's grosso modo twenty minutes walking to the *rue Pierre Marchant* and then through the deserted streets of Anderlecht to the boulevard Sylvain Dupuis. This quest will harden the body, while the brisk breeze stiffens the clothes.

On the boulevard, hail one of these Taxis Bleus. Get your story ready: *Man, what a party! Jumped rat-assed drunk with all my clothes on into the swimming pool. Freezing, man, I tell you, my balls almost fell off, but I was the star of the evening. So sorry for the smell—the pool hadn't been cleaned for two months.*

The body dreams of the warm softness of a soapy bath.

The body thinks: *Birgit will cry a river when she hears about her daughter.*

Tja. Life is a bitch and then you…

The body thinks: *Why am I so fucking alone?*

***

You dream of me while I'm crouching on your dick, Drees.
You gasp, but you don't feel a thing.
Shed my leading role in your nightmare. Wake up and move that old man's

body.

> *Don't lie there snoring in your bed with your mouth wide open.*
> *Your closed eyes don't fool me.*
> *You're awake and you can still feel my presence, can't you?*
> *You have killed me to take revenge on my father.*
> *Get up.*
> *Do your thing.*
> *Grab the phone.*
> *Dial the number 0.*
> *When a woman picks up, start breathing through your nose.*
> *The woman, a grieving mother, shouts at you, wants to know who you are.*
> *You want to tell her what you did.*
> *You can't.*
> *You breathe.*
> *She slams down the phone.*
> *Your finger creeps toward the redial button…*
> *There… there you go, Drees…*
> *Only the sound of breathing and the thumping of your heart…*

The Left Hand Path of Tantra

1

*T*he Seventies boring, dull, and gray?

Not for Johnny Di Machio, plagued by dreams of being raped, followed by mirages of twinkling and rattling COMSATS in the outer layers of the atmosphere. Johnny was convinced that these scientific marvels were destined to ignite the wrath of legions of nuclear missiles any minute now, and right above his head.

His lonely existence in chaotic and brazen Antwerp, the Flemish harbor-city he was living in, drove Johnny Di Machio to keeping a diary. He jotted down personal stuff in third person and wasn't averse to some effortless, often ludicrous, rhyming. *Johnny and Death, two peas in a pot of meth. Johnny and Love, abandoned by that precious dove.*

Writing down these observations, Johnny was grievously aware that he would never be a writer, one of his daydreams along with captain of an ice-breaker, keeper of a lighthouse, and, the all-time-classic for young, self-destructive males, a guardian of an Arabic prince's harem.

On rainy days, Johnny di Machio imagined himself fleeing the world's impending nuclear destruction to set up residence in Mongolia, where, in the evenings, he would squat before his *gers* and watch his horse graze peacefully. The noble animal would sleep next to him in the tent at night, when the steppe was breathing ice and *Equus'* spicy heat was welcome. The steed alternated sleeping lying and standing, so Johnny had to be careful not to be crushed. The broomtail liked a bale of hay about every four hours, so Johnny's daydream-nights were filled plenty. In spite of all these inconveniences, the serene chomping of the Messenger between the Worlds, as the Mongolians call their horses, was like a lullaby of yore in Johnny's ears, a relic from an innocent childhood.

But all Johnny's fantasies, fears, and fobbing, didn't annihilate that one fatal question: why did he often suffer from nightmares of being raped in his native village by a mentally retarded thirteen-year-old neighbor when he himself had been around ten?

2

When Johnny di Machio didn't fantasize about Mongolia, his melodramatic death at Nuclear Doomsday, or the retarded neighbor-boy's balls, he kept himself busy scribbling in his weepy diary about a girl whom he called Blondie, a sprightly maiden who winked at him now and then when she came to buy fashion magazines in the bookstore where Johnny was a clerk. *Blondie, all butter and cream, Blondie, all sugar and spice, you know what I mean, and, ooohh, man, she's nice.*

Mjam mjam, Johnny couldn't help thinking every time she sailed past him toward the magazine-stand. *I'll tell her straight-a-way: you are so mjam mjam!* But before he had mustered the courage to mouth this smashing compliment, Blondie had wrapped the local bad guy—his nickname in Antwerp was Fornicating Frankie, go figure—around her finger, and also in her lower regions, what resulted in a ruddy baby of the male sex, who, in turn, resulted in Frankie's embarking, like a "lubricated fart" one heard him say, on an oil-tanker destined for distant seas.

It didn't take Blondie ages to distribute tantalizing signs that she was honestly, so help me God, convinced that Johnny Di Machio would be a worthy husband and a doting stepfather for her love child. She chose with care her shortest skirt and highest heels, and rang Johnny's bell.

Johnny didn't object.

His parents had taught him to be obedient.

***

"I'm a girl of expensive taste," said Blondie, five minutes after she had moved in, while inspecting Johnny's bathroom. "In wining, in dining, and in all jewels worth the mining."

She turned, exposing her décolleté.

One glance at Johnny's glassy eyes was enough.

He was hers; him and his purse.

3

Johnny di Machio was a bookstore salesman with an eclectic taste. Equipped with opinions he'd picked up from Sunday Literary Supplements he tried to sell Fernando Pessoa's verses to Stephen King-devotees. His boss continuously threatened to fire him. When Johnny came home, tired, unsatisfied, and sad because no one had followed his advice to read André Baillon or Curzio Malaparte, he clacked his Mongolian prayer-rattles for at least an hour, an activity that provoked banshee-like cries in Blondie's son—now also *his* son, she insisted.

In short, Blondie very soon turned from lust to load. The moment came in which she stopped kissing the toad. Prince Di Machio had evaporated somewhere along the line. Searching for a solution, Johnny read during his working hours books of Mongolian monks with unspeakable names that were stashed eons ago in the outer universe of the bookstore, the shelves underneath the staircase. They advised him to dump his Self in order to become the Will-less Nothingness, a rather overworked expression in Johnny's style-sensitive eyes, but tempting nevertheless. Johnny Will-less Nothingness, at your service.

All this Nothingness made Johnny very thirsty after a while, so he developed the habit to get, after a day's work with no sales, schnuckered on brandy of dubious provenance in various stages of intensity before he weltered, singing frayed shanties, towards home, where a bleating, red-faced little demon was waiting for him, in team with a nagging wife whose elfin eyes had since long turned into black overall-buttons.

4

April. April 9, 1976, to be precise.

(At this stage, I have to tell you between parentheses that the quays of Antwerp are picturesque; don't forget to visit them when you come over, along with hordes of Chinese tourists.)

Anyway, the quays were the reason why a voice behind Johnny's right shoulder answered his call "I'm flying high as a kite!" to no-one in particular in his hangout café *Den Bonten Os,* with:"And fly you will from the nearest quay, lad, but I predict: not as a kite."

Johnny quacked deafeningly. A side-splitter and a knee-slapper in one!

He turned around.

And faced Fornicating Frankie who gave him the stink-eye, thus reducing him from Johnny di Machio to Johnny di Minusio.

***

Normally, it's highly amusing to describe a fight between two males, but when one is heated-up, and the other is a half-drunk coward, one has to put up with degrading sensations, like the sound of defenseless meat being slapped, primeval grunts (produced by Fornicating Frankie) and high-pitched wails (emitted by Johnny di Machio).

But wait! A bearded person clad in a wide, orange shirt, revealing lots of chest hair and a *mandala,* stepped in, and grabbed Frankie by the arm. Frankie reacted with what he always did in dire circumstances like this one: a right hook, *bamm,* aimed directly at the man's jaw.

Oh, but it wasn't there anymore, the man's jaw. Pivoting on his right foot, the orange guy slapped Frankie with a loose, almost waving gesture in the face. The result was literally staggering: Frankie was thrown against the bar, blood seeping from his nose.

"I suggest you leave," the stranger said to Frankie. Johnny scanned the pub with alcohol-glazed eyes. Where were the cameras? This had to be a scene from some Kung Fu street-fighter movie, wow, and the special effects were mind-staggering!

Frankie was not one to give up. He struggled to his feet, pulled his head in like a turtle, and revved up, ready to deliver his famous, devastating head-butt. The mandala-wearer swung his body aside gracefully, his arms flaying, delivering puny-looking slaps in a hellish tempo on Frankie's neck and face. The result was a total collapse of the seasoned street-fighter. *Finito la musica.* It became very quiet in the joint.

The bearded man turned to Johnny di Machio. Pale as a ghost, Johnny whispered: "I'm so sorry I can't fight, but, you see, I was abused when I was ten!" It was the same lie that he'd conjured up years ago when his *mojo* didn't work on that fateful first night with his first naked girl: "I'm so sorry I can't do it, but, you see, I was abused when I was ten!"

"If you can't fight other men, learn to fight with yourself," the beard answered. "I'll teach you, aided by the psychic power of my guru Bhagwan Sri Rajneesh."

Oh yeah, this was Antwerp, where loonies were the norm. Johnny nodded eagerly.

5

It was dawn before Johnny showed up at his apartment. Until this point in his life, entropy had reined.

Now, entropy had left the building; chaos stepped in.

Johnny, sweaty, and feeling euphoric after a night of listening to the famous Indian guru Baghwan Sri Rajneesh's videoed speeches about illumination and other yummy concepts during a gathering of Antwerp devotees, followed by dancing in the nude with a horde of guys and gals, getting loose, reaching "the bottom of the ego-pit," as Isiro, the bearded one, Johnny's Savior, had called the suggestive shaking limbs and pelvises of the crowd. Afterwards came the licking, the pushing and shoving, the grunting, the smells of lust, body-slamming in all kinds of positions, and Johnny in a corner, staring at the bottom of the ego-pit, wrestling exciting revulsion for rich female armpit-and-pubic-hair.

When he left at about six a.m., Isiro hugged him, reeking of "the holy substance of life," wine, and sweat.

"Do like I did," Isiro said. "Travel to Poona, learn to become a free spirit, rejoice in the spiritual light of Baghwan's wisdom. Shed your old skin."

He looked quizzically at Johnny. "Don't be afraid." He brought his face nearer. "Why didn't you join in the carnage? Sexual problems can be overcome in Poona when you follow rebirth, followed by the path of tantric sexual bliss."

Johnny blurted out a colorful story of his poor, tragically raped ten-year-old rump. He had rehearsed this heart-blasting tale frantically in his corner during the orgy, knowing he would need it to shield himself from the shame of his sexual inhibition. But the story he told was different from what he had concocted, more violent, literally stuffed with details.

If that was not proof that he *really* suffered from lifelong, sexual PTSD, what was?

"Throw yourself in the arms of your fate, my friend," Isiro said, hugging him a last time. "Tantric bliss is your remedy, Poona is your destiny! Learn how to become a fearless lover!"

***

Johnny had walked home with a bounce in his step, but now he stood, heavy as sourdough, in the bedroom of his apartment, absently listening to Blondie's icy scolding, soon accompanied by her little demon's wailing. Johnny deliberated, for a second, to give Blondie a good pounding, aided by all the images of the past hours whirling in his mind.

Sensing the vinegar smell of contempt emanating from the blanketed lump on the bed, he went to the kitchen instead, drank three cups of instant coffee, and left for his work.

That day, he didn't persuade any bookstore customer to read Kafka's collected works. He was too busy searching in the cobweb-ridden corners of the store for instruction manuals about Tantra. He found none.

When he came home at a quarter past five, Blondie's closet was bare, the little demon's room was barren, and his bank account had suffered a deadly onslaught.

On the kitchen table, a note: *Frankie is back, you hack: Frankie is thrice the man you'll ever be, you mouse, you louse, you grouse. Nevermore will I want to see you, goodbye and toodeloo!*

Johnny sighed. The note's style made him wonder if Blondie had been reading in his diary behind his back.

He looked out of the window. It rained.

Maybe it was time to learn how to become a fearless lover.

6

Guesthouse Sunderban in Poona had been the property of a Bengalese prince in the nineteenth century. Afterwards, the mansion fell into the hands of an English family. The rooms, upholstered with polished edible wood, made a great impression on Johnny.

He rented one of them. The manager, an unreliable-looking toad with an eternal trickle of Betel juice along his mouth corners, told him that one of the daughters of the Bengalese prince, an outstanding beauty who had been kidnapped by a Lebanese slave trader, rose every morning as a warm mist from the garden and made her rounds in the rooms.

"Surely, a sensitive man like you, a student of the Great Rajneesh, will see her one night," the owner concluded and spat bethel juice. "When you see a moving pole of light with a halo of red, then you'll know it's her."

Johnny smiled politely. "Is she nice?"

The owner spat again. "Ghosts, young man, are not nice. They are vindictive and want to feed on the energy of your soul. Ghosts and ghouls are one and the same."

***

Johnny's first night in his Sunderban room was filled with tossing and turning under his mosquito net. He had read somewhere that a first night in a strange bed released predictive powers. And lo and behold, behind his closed eyes, he saw Blondie running away from him on a rainy path. He yearned to call her, but was too afraid: he could feel Fornicating Frankie waiting for him in ambush.

In his half-sleep Johnny cried bitter essences of anxiety and remorse. So mighty was his torrent of sadness that the gaseous remains of the Bengalese princess became attracted to him. When she floated into his room, Johnny's body began to prickle from head to toe. The spooky presence didn't speak; speech was an ability she had lost. It didn't matter: Johnny's body reacted adequately. An undulation became visible in the sheets, his loins fired up a rocket.

Was it his dream-imagination, or did he really hear the subtle rasping of a gold bull beetle in his room, producing a sound that resonated like: *Johnny, poor Johnny, lonesome Johnny, violated Johnny?*

7

"Baksheesh," the little boy with the sad, squinting eyes implored. He

huddled like a broken doll in a roughly constructed wooden cart. It resembled the cart that 5-year-old Johnny used to pull up and down on the street before his elders' house, singing to himself: *dikke poep-dikke poep-oepededoepedoep! (Fat ass—fat ass- yessayessayaaasss)* Johnny wore goofy knickerbockers that showed the fat rolls on his thighs, a sign that he was a child well taken care off.

The Indian child had no fleshy legs.

He had none.

The miniature Indian beggar repeated his plea. Johnny looked over the boy's head at Sunderban's spicy gardens that he had just left. Ten paces on the street, and already a dilemma. What was the right thing to do? The boy yanked at Johnny's trousers, and repeated his prayer. An Indian fellowman, wearing a grandiose yellow turban, passed and kicked the cart. The tiny beggar retreated, pushing his cart with swift crab-like movements of his arms, aiming a pathetic look over his shoulder at Johnny. Johnny noticed that the Indian fellowman wore an emerald in his tie. He felt relieved and angry at the same time, so he stuck out his neck and told the Indian that he could decide on his own when to give baksheesh or not. The Indian fellowman shook his head. What an ignoramus, this European buffoon! He jutted out his lower lip and hissed, "Be careful. Some parents chop off a leg for more baksheesh."

"You are kidding me," Johnny said. "Are you kidding me?"

"You heard what I said, sir. You want to buy dope? I have prime dope."

Johnny refused politely. The Indian looked at him lugubriously, moved his head in a horizontal figure eight, and went on.

"What a bleedin' apple tart, the bugger," a voice behind Johnny said.

Johnny turned around. A small, bow-legged white guy with huge black sunglasses on his wax-pale face stood behind him, dressed in an orange robe, wearing a mandala.

The newcomer spat behind the Indian's back, and shouted "Ooohh, he's got his clements on!" The Indian looked over his shoulders, and doubled the speed of his steps. The sunglasses-guy turned to Johnny who caught a whiff of overheated tarmac and brandy on his breath. "Should'a kicked him in the bleedin' brown cobblers, mate!"

***

Alan Berr turned out to be a cockney from east London. In the five minutes' walk from Sanderban to Bhagwan's ashram, Alan taught Johnny di Machio that 'clements' were hemorrhoids—after which he gave a detailed explanation of his own—that an "apple tart" was a fart, and "cobblers" were balls. Alan refused to acknowledge that his brand new friend—"Roast me, a bleedin' Flemin'!"- didn't understand much of his dialect. Consequently, he treated Johnny as a retarded five-year-old, and considered it his duty to give him a tour of Bhagwan's ashram, a sun-blistered collection of bizarre brownstone buildings, sailcloth tents, and jungle. At the entrance, they had to pass a guard with a gigantic Afro-coupe. Alan made a few rude jokes about dogs and Indians not allowed, and in they were. Johnny was soon mesmerized by the cacophony of sights, sounds, and smells, while Allan dragged him along from the central Buddha-hall where, in the evenings, Bhagwan addressed the questions of his devotees, to smaller buildings where numerous therapies—one was dervish-dancing—were going on.

Feeling quite dizzy because of Alan's rollercoaster manners, Johnny was led to the ashram's administration center, and paid a heart-stopping sum to be admitted as an apprentice for five days. An orange robe was mandatory in the commune. Alan accompanied him to the robe-store, chose the right size for Johnny's lanky frame, and then abruptly went off for a "bleedin' primal therapy session with some Ballroom Blitz fannies!"

"What's that?" Johnny hollered after him.

"See for yourself, y'old wanker!" was the answer.

Despite his bow-legs, Alan was remarkably quick on his feet.

***

Johnny wandered through the ashram and encountered groups of laughing, chatting, music-making, dancing people who took no notice of him. A bunch of men and women were splashing around naked in a big shallow pond. No-one invited him in or called him a voyeur. The atmosphere in the commune reminded him of a documentary he'd seen about the Woodstock festival. He felt the urge to skedaddle growing in him, like so many years ago during his first day in primary school. A panicked madness of loneliness had taken hold of him when an inner voice gleefully whispered that his mother would not return to pick him up, as she had promised. Johnny became berserk, and started shrieking, screaming, and wailing. The other kids were delighted; the teacher shook him by the shoulders and told him not to be a natty-boy. On the ashram's main cross-road, natty-boy Johnny stood stock-still, and slammed his hands on his ears, shaking his head like a madman.

Shrieks from the encounter-group on his right.

Screams from the primal therapy-group on his left.

Wailing from the rebirth-group in front of him.

These awful sounds of healing were offered to the grand picture of Rajneesh Bhagwan, hanging in the central, egg-formed Buddha-hall. The ashram was the Theater of New Mankind, but Johnny was like a Yeti on a far mountaintop, longing for, but lost to, humanity.

Exhausted, he sat on the grass between the shrubs and the palm trees of a small arbor.

"*Een fijne dag, nietwaar, leerling?*" (*A fine day, isn't it, apprentice?*)

For the second time that day, someone had spoken behind Johnny's back, this time not in cockney, but in Dutch. A replica of a Christ-head, screwed on a skinny and high rise frame, stood behind him in an orange robe with a white sash around his hips. The Christ-head introduced himself as *sannyasin* Arup, and told Johnny he was the liaison for all the Dutch people in the ashram.

"I'm not Dutch, I'm Flemish," Johnny said.

"Ah, I can sense a well-developed sense of identity, my friend. Small people have a tendency to flaunt it, and that can cause problems. No worries, you'll lose it here."

Johnny immediately disliked the other's self-assurance. "I always heard that Dutch people have an *over-developed* sense of identity. Did you lose it here?"

The Christ-head scowled benignly. "Haw, haw, that's a good one. I meant that nationality doesn't exist here. We're all Bhagwan's children, nurtured by the aura of his Buddha field."

"Okay. But being Flemish is, as far as I know, nowhere a problem, and I'm not a Bhagwan-child yet."

"Are all Flemings so sarcastic, even a bit aggressive? You must excuse me; you're the first one that I've met."

"Flemings are generally shy, "Johnny said demurely.

"Why then aren't you?"

"I just arrived an hour ago. I used all my savings for this trip; it's very important for me to *learn* something here, to do this right. But the atmosphere of this place makes me feel small and puny."

"That's good. You first have to *un-learn* before you can learn your own worth."

"I read stuff like that in Bhagwan's books," Johnny said, wondering why he felt so reckless. "And a whole lot of other feathery philosophy. That's not my reason for coming."

"Pray, what may then be your reason?"

"I can't tell you. It's rather personal. I want to tell it to Bhagwan himself. I must be able to look him in the eye."

"We all want that. Not many of us get a chance."

"I am a well-known journalist in Belgium. If I'm not satisfied when I go back, I could write a very abrasive story about life in this commune." Johnny's mind raced. He had booked for five days. It had been much more expensive than in the folders he had read. That meant he would be on a plane back to Brussels before the commune would find out—if they went to the trouble of researching him—that he wasn't a famous Belgian journalist at all.

Arup threw Johnny a piercing look. "Your mind is obviously out of balance. I sense a dark entity in you. You hide an evil secret, my friend. I could ask the Master if he wants you to follow a special kind of cleansing. When you comply, you could be a candidate for a private session."

"Besides being a journalist," Johnny went on, hot-headed by the apparent success of his bluff, "I also own a bookshop in Antwerp, run by my wife. I sell a lot of Bhagwan's books in Dutch translation."

Arup patted Johnny on the back, and said that, in that case, Bhagwan would be in touch with personal counsel for his cleansing very soon.

***

Two hours later, back in Sunderban's garden, wandering around the trees, Johnny wondered why he always lied when he was confronted with people who acted superior. With his pen-knife, he started carving Blondie's name in a camphor tree.

Did he miss her?

Why did he so unexpectedly miss her that much?

During their five months partnership, he had never told Blondie that he had been violently raped by the thirteen-year-old dim-witted son of the neighbors. Not even when his bedroom-Johnny refused to be a prick on many nights, and Blondie started to ogle him with some distaste.

He didn't want to repeat that stale old lie to her.

So he'd told her that his pelvis' nerve-machinery had been damaged in a car-accident when he was ten.

No dramatic problem for Blondie, who liked sleeping anyway.

Maybe he should have told her the truth.

Chances were it had happened after all, the violation, the rape, the profanation.

Violent sex, endured at a tender age.

Johnny, a rabbit page for the moron's flesh-sword.

Sex and fear united in a single howl, a unique tone.

Johnny, beggarly Johnny, turned into cold stone.

Why was there no mercy on him, oh Lord?

8

The next morning, Sanderban's owner spat a glob of bethel juice in front of Johnny's feet and handed him a note. Johnny opened it and saw it was Bhagwan's choice for his cleansing.

The Master's decision was short: *The Left Hand Path Of Tantra.*

Johnny felt his stomach tighten and remembered he hadn't eaten since noon yesterday.

In the breakfast room—the disinfectants' stink there could get an elephant high—Alan Berr slumped in front of a bowl of ghastly English porridge. The Londoner scarcely looked up when Johnny said good morning, and didn't answer. Cautiously, Johnny crossed the room, sat down at a far-corner table, and ordered his breakfast almost in a whisper. He had swallowed his first spoonful of ants-sweet gruel, when Alan stood up and started to recite in an exalted voice.

Hear ye, I didn't swallow a golden lock
it was an iron moon I ingested too soon.
The wee lads, bent over their machine-cock
perish before they taste the grapes of passion.
I quaffed the rush; was wolfed down by a loon
Chugalug of various kinds sprang from my throat
In one lump of Will Divine, a gush of action:
Revenge will and shall be mine, hear my oath….

Johnny saw the two waiters in the dining room exchange glances. He rose from his chair and clapped. Alan squinted at him as if Johnny was a creature from deep space, mumbled something, tried to get from behind his table, collapsed. Tablecloth and cutlery clattered in shards on the floor. In their haste to get to the table, the waiters bumped into each other.

A fat Indian fellowman followed by a fat Indian fellow-woman and three mini-fatties marched into the dining room. Like gooses in a row, they stared at Alan, their eyes small, black buttons in their puffed-up faces. The waiters tried to steer Alan to the door. He shook them off.

"I am the working-class bard!" he roared. "I'm the poet of rock-hard factory facts! Get your slimy paws off me, you turd, you piece of lard!"

Johnny wiped his mouth with his napkin, and walked over. "Please," he said to the struggling Indian fellowmen, "be careful with my friend. I'm a bookshop owner in Antwerp, Belgium. This gentle-man is a famous poet whom I would like to publish. A bit eccentric, I can't deny, but aren't all great artists?"

Everyone stared at him, even Alan whose black glasses hung askew on his nose.

Johnny was shocked by the bulbous opaque blue orb where Alan's left eye should have been.

***

After some wrangling, and an intervention of the hotel owner, Johnny and Alan found themselves on the street, ready for their daily pilgrim-age to the ashram. The sun's glare was so intense, it was blinding, deaf-ening, and maddening.

"Thanks, guv, you're a blast," said Alan. "It is the first time that someone calls me 'a great artist' instead of a gipsy's kiss, or a frog and toad."

Johnny felt two sinewy arms around his neck and was pulled for-ward until his and Alan's forehead touched each other: "Just call Alan if you want someone's head butted on this rancid soil," the Londoner whispered, and then he was gone, leaving behind the prickly sensation of his stubbly kiss on Johnny's left cheek, and a distinct aura of gin-and-tonic.

Bob Van Laerhoven

9

Johnny was eager to show the Dutch *sannyasin* Arup that, although they had a false start the day before, he was a polite and sensible young man without any demonic ties or reins. He paid without sarcastic remarks for a five days' course of *Left Hand Path Tantra* with Ma Sarita, according to Arup "the best sexual teacher we have."

Despite all his good intentions, Johnny couldn't help remarking that he felt guilty. Here he was, in this lush ashram, paying for his fulfillment, while outside the commune, the homeless and the street kids were perishing in the dark soot of the exhausts of countless Tata-trucks.

"It's their karma," Arup responded, "and it is your mission in life to search for the way the furnaces of your body link physical love to self-hatred, victimhood, violence, death, and occult beings in the night."

Johnny peered at the Dutchman, trying to remember what lies he had told Arup yesterday about his sexuality. He couldn't, but he suspected they were not the smartest he had ever told.

10

"A fearful person needs to jump into the heart of terror itself before he's able to transmute it," Ma Sarita pontificated. The German Tantric teacher was a brown-haired, small, well-curved woman. Something in her physical make-up reminded Johnny of Janis Joplin.

"In defiance of all the beautiful words we use to describe love," Ma Sarita went on in her clipped German accent, "fear is much more universal. It causes our existence to be devoid of real consciousness. The more anxiety, the more alienation. Tell me, Johnny, do you sometimes suffer from the feeling that someone else is leading your existence?"

Johnny swallowed, hesitated, and looked away.

Ma Sarita smiled. She had strong, slightly bent teeth. "That someone is fear's brother… Bhagwan calls him The Shadow."

Johnny narrowed his eyes. This was a foreboding beginning, in his book. That woman went too fast and was too smart.

"I call him The Liar," he said.

After hours of Bhagwan's philosophical theories followed by Ohmmm-mming together, Johnny sat naked on his knees in front of Ma Sarita, who, small and supple as she was, felt suddenly imposing in her orange robe. Johnny was so skittish that his rod had shrunk to the size of a peanut.

"Now tell me why it is so hard for you to have sex."

"It's so hard because my Johnny—Johnny pointed at his scrotum—often isn't hard enough."

Ma Sarita smiled. "At least, you can joke about it."

"I'm joking out of despair. My psychiatrist has ruled that I am hypersensitive, hypochondriac, and narcissistic. I can only consider sex when I pity a woman." Johnny started to stutter. "But that frame of mind is a trap, because whom do I pity? Physically unattractive women. Therefore, I don't feel great lust when it comes down to have sex with them, and the outcome tends to be, ehh, substandard."

While he was twaddling this theory, Johnny's despair had grown. What should've been a believable and intricate lie with a shitload of psychological layers had become a stuttering mishmash. Where was his talent to tell *inspired* lies, shrewd, theatrical, even thespian?

Scolding himself, he lowered his gaze disapprovingly at his peanut. Ma Sarita put with one swift movement her hand on his crotch. Johnny felt in his marrow and bones how true the expression *private parts* were. The touch of Ma Sarita's fingers boiled his cullions.

"Your genitals tell me that you're not telling the truth," Ma Sarita said.

It took long seconds, but then Johnny bowed his head like a worshipper who begs for absolution of his sins.

"Don't think you can fool me, Johnny," Sarita went on. "The Left Hand Path of Tantra is an ordeal. Every secret that you're hiding damages you. You have to bring it to the surface. The battle will be arduous; you're here for a no-holds-barred fight with yourself. There are certain social limits to programs for sexual healing in the West, but not here, not in Our Master's sphere of influence."

Johnny nodded timidly.

The Watcher in him wanted to slap her.

The Shadow in him wanted to bite her throat.

The Liar in him wanted her to feel what he felt.

The Lover in him wanted to cry.

11

After two days of sessions with the curly Tantric teacher, Johnny found it harder to remember all the things he lied about, but even more difficult to hide the violence underneath his shyness. Ma Sarita never seemed afraid or concerned. She laid her hands on his body when he became trapped in heinous sexual fantasies, or banged like a berserk warrior of bygone times on the boxing bag in one corner of her therapy room. Afterwards, Johnny wondered if she knew that he'd wanted to hit *her*.

For the moment, her water was stronger than his fire.

After three days, he told her things he remembered of the abuse he had suffered, and then things he had forgotten. Afterwards, he wondered if he had spoken the truth. He'd attempted to lie as usual, but it had become burdensome for no apparent reason.

At last, he told her about seeing a golem in his dreams from as long as he could remember.

It was a shock to him when he realized he had spoken the truth.

"A golem with a face of clay?"

"I can't see his face. He's huge... Like a sumo-wrestler."

"Who is he?" Ma Sarita stood up. Suddenly, she seemed a threat to Johnny.

"The one who..." Johnny said. "The one who...." His voice faltered. A mad drummer banged a solo in his throat. *What was going on?*

"Shut your eyes and put your right hand on your heart."

Johnny grimaced, but he obeyed as the meek child he had been.

"Now, try to see the golem's face."

Johnny swallowed.

"Tell him what you've wanted to say to him all along."

A malicious look appeared on Johnny's face. At last, Ma Sarita saw his Shadow, a dominant and maleficent demon, a lonely winter king in a far-away ice-palace.

"Cannot. His eyes, so black," Johnny said in a voice that yodeled as if he was a Yeti on a high mountain top again, *sad Johnny, lonesome Johnny, bronco Johnny, walker Johnny.* "I wanted to stop him, but those eyes..."

"Look into those black eyes," Ma Sarita said.

"I knew what he was intending…" Johnny sighed and shuddered, *Johnny of the seven seas, Johnny of the burning bush, Johnny of the weeping heart.*

"What was the golem about and to whom?" Ma Sarita said.

Johnny opened his eyes and looked at her. Sarita recognized the green wolf-light in those eyes. A small bell lay within her reach on a table. If Johnny attacked her, two sturdy *sannyasins* would come to her call.

"Nothing," Johnny said. He hunched his shoulders. "The golem is just a nightmare from my youth."

Ma Sarita knew that this abrupt mental retreat meant she was close to his secret. Hovering around Johnny, she saw the shimmer of a spoiled sorrow, like a trace of moldy bread crumbs left in a dark forest long time ago, *dark Johnny, Johnny of the thousand kisses, Johnny of the bleeding heart.*

12

Excerpt of Johnny's diary: entry from that evening.

9 September 1976

Oh Lord Omnipotent, save Swami Johnny-yoki from Flanders.

Holy Gent, Swami Johnny-yoki from Flanders is flabbergasted.

Swami Johnny-yoki from Flanders almost betrayed his deepest secret.

Swami Johnny-yoki from Flanders wants to vanish.

Back to the teat and into the womb.

It was good dawdling to the teat and into the womb for Swami Johnny-yoki from Flanders.

The rest was drivel and thunder, and all kinds of bragging and kickbacks.

In the womb-tomb, Swami Johnny-yoki from Flanders was better off than in the existential realm filled with penitence and clemency.

That says Swami Johnny-yoki from Flanders, master liar, flesh-friar who once succumbed to the power of the moron dick.

13

That night, the Bengalese princess-ghost reappeared more condensed than ever in Johnny's Sunderban-bedroom. In his minefield between sleep and wakefulness, Johnny dreamed about soldiers, disguised as monks, attacking his village, pilfering the houses, torching the men, raping the women.

In his dream-state, he was a thirteen-year-old girl with a large copper-colored birthmark on her right thigh. When he realized this, a chill crept up his spine and immobilized him, unable to flee from the rapist who materialized in the darkest of dark.

A silver bell tingled close to his right ear.

On her toes, as a prima ballerina, the princess came to Johnny's mosquito-net to rescue him from his nightmare. She wrapped herself around the net and inspected him with huge amber eyes, in which he saw himself reflected.

She was so serene, so young, so green—and so well-proportioned—that, once more, Johnny's love-brush went rigid underneath the clammy sheet.

Please, don't hurt me because I was a coward and didn't try to save her, Johnny broadcasted to the princess. He pulled the sheet over his head and hissed like the *nahash,* the serpent of desire and cunning in Eden, when he remembered in full clarity and detail how the golem had ravished the first girl he had ever loved.

14

The next day, Ma Sarita had to admit that Johnny's Shadow was cunning. He changed course easier than a scorpion and put a lot of contradictory avowals in Johnny's mouth. She knew she had to find something powerful to break through Johnny's defenses.

"I've never felt *right* as a man," was one of the Shadow's new tricks. "I'd rather been a woman. That's why sex is such a burden to me."

"Okay, in that case, I'll fuck you," Ma Sarita answered bluntly. "But you must look the part. Put it away."

Johnny looked at her in the way a patient ox in a rice field beholds the horizon.

"Put your penis between your legs," she explained. "I'll show you." Sarita turned Johnny on his belly and gently arranged his balls and penis between his thighs. With an energetic hop, she then threw herself on him, splashed with her lower belly on his ass like a fish on the dry, groaned, rolled her eyes, and panted vehemently. She pinched Johnny's nipples; she blew her breath in his ears. She ground her hips as if she needed to tame a bucking horse.

After a final grunt that carried all the signs of accomplishment, she ushered a few mighty sighs, and lay still.

Amused, Johnny said, "Go on."

Ma Sarita shot him a dubious glance. "Why? I just came!"

Johnny laughed for the first time since she met him, but Ma Sarita noticed that it wasn't a liberating guffaw.

"Now that I've fucked you, tell me what you feel," she said.

"It was... funny."

"Yes, when I stopped. But your body was tense the whole way through."

"It was...weird."

"Yes, and you became angry. I could feel it in your aura."

"I wasn't afraid."

"No, part of your brain still remembered it was me, small, cute Ma Sarita. Another part remembered the time when it was not small, cute Ma Sarita. I saw the muscles of your neck tense."

Silence.

"I hate you," Johnny said. "Oh, I hate you so." He grabbed her by the shoulders and pushed her on the yoga-mats.

She felt his erection against her labia, and glanced at her little bell but waited. Eye to eye they were, him on top of her, their genitals touching. Then, his eyes misted over, and she knew he had retreated again.

"I have an English friend in hotel Sunderban," he whispered. "He told me he is here to fight the aggression he feels against women. I'll ask him what *he* would do, if he was lying underneath you with his dick cockled between his thighs and you humping him."

15

That evening, Johnny, a sucker for distraction, was reading a novel of the Flemish author Louis Paul Boon—a Noble Prize candidate according to the patriotic Flemish Press. His eyes had reached the sentence "*Only the hope to reach that cunt, to press my mouth against it, to make her hot and to lie upon her, made me accept everything she did*" when there was a loud knock on the door.

The Bengalese princess turned into living flesh with a bottle of bubbles? Johnny opened the door with a slight tremor in his spine.

"I want you to come with me," Alan said. The hued light of the corridor exploded in his dark glasses like a miniature gas giant in a distant galaxy. "I have to show you something and need your help."

Johnny retreated a few steps into the safety of his room. As in a ballet, Alan followed him fluently. "You understood my poems," he said, his Cockney-accent strangely gone. "You saw the gleam of the artist in me, the working class poet, writing about machines that rip young people apart in the factory where I work. You showed *soul* yesterday morning. And you own a book shop."

"I don't exactly own…"

"I will tell you what happened to me today." Alan rubbed his forehead savagely. "And then you have to accompany me."

Johnny realized that the sweaty and grimy Londoner was quite drunk or stoned, or both.

In spite of this—or just because of that—Alan told Johnny a heartbreaking tale.

16

I hankered to learn how it feels to love. That's why I travelled all the way— I puke in planes!—to this Bhagwan-bloke. I wanted to know how it feels when I show myself to a woman like I genuinely am.

And what did I get? Hullabaloo-mystics, jaunty stories about soul-retrieving practices to become intact again, and cuddle-sessions with flaky people while we were lying on our backs with our toes touching each other, yechh, annoyed by the teacher bleating some dim-witted parable about a carpet that spun itself.

Do you know the parable of the carpet that spun itself, Johnny? No? Well, that is a real shame for your incomplete soul. I'll tell you the parable; you'll feel a lot better afterwards.

Listen here: the carpet that spun itself hovered a few centimeters above the ground and spun every thread it could find. Because it didn't think its endeavor through, it soon became a gigantic mess. It just spun and spun itself. Soon, it resembled a rag that was created by a retarded child. It had all colors of the rainbow, and a slew of materials: grass and hay, dog hairs, leaves and thorns, and discarded ropes and ribbons and such. It spun and it spun until it was quite a pitiable sight.

One morning, the carpet that spun itself met a pool of water, and the first sun turned it into a mirror. The carpet saw its image and was shocked. It became so disgusted with itself that it hid away in an old house. Every morning, it crept up the stairs crying and wailing, searching for beauty. But it only gathered dust. The stairs wore out the carpet fast—every morning, it became more berserk in its search. After a while, it was in frazzles, and so lonely that its wails became banshee-cries. Nobody dared to enter the old house anymore. The forlorn yowling that could be heard going up the stairs, just before daybreak each morning, was proof that the house was haunted big time.

There was almost nothing left of the carpet, when, finally, a man entered. He wasn't afraid of ghosts; he wanted to end his life. He hoped to find something to commit suicide with in that old house. He searched the cellar and found nothing. He searched all rooms, and was disappointed. But then he came onto the attic where he saw the last shreds of the carpet lying spent on the ground.

There was just enough fabric left for him to weave a noose, and with it, he managed to exhale his last breath.

***

"I asked the guy in front, a half-assed *sannyasin*, the meaning of his ludicrous story." Alan, sitting cross-legged on the floor, with Johnny on the sofa in front of him, had become quite agitated while he was telling the parable of the carpet that spun itself. "The blubber looked at me in an odd way. I didn't realize it, but by that time I was plucking at the grass between my knees. I never plucked grass before. Instead of answering my question, the moron bawled with that posh accent of his, "Apprentice, if you wish to become a cow, I'm afraid your place isn't here. I love grass, and I ask you kindly to leave it alone."

"I jumped to my feet, said he could go and fuck himself, and if he was too measly-assed to do that, I would be obliged to butt-plug him myself. The miser just smiled and shook his head. I should have banged his skull in right there, but I still cherished the faint hope that, if I was patient enough, I would at last *learn* something. But I also knew I needed to vent off steam, so I headed straight out of that madhouse, looking for a drink and a fight....

"I think I found both, because hours later, I came to myself in one of Poona's shady quarters with my shirt in tatters, and couldn't remember how I got there..."

***

The street was an uppercut of stinking buses, Tata-taxi's, motorized rickshaws, and humongous Lorries. Four rickshaw-drivers were pulling my sleeves. I didn't remember Sunderban's address or the name of the joint. I clearly saw the hotel in my mind's eye, but that was all. One of the drivers had a balloon face sitting on a skeletal body. I saw that full moon face double, and both were surrounded by a violet hue. I found it very interesting, as if I was speaking to a ghost.

"Take me somewhere where I can have a stiff drink," I said. *"Understood?"*

"Bangla?" he said.

"Whatever you call it, but it has to be hard liquor, no beer-piss."

The man pointed to his rickshaw. I stepped in; shut my eyes. Wow, so dizzy that I was. Before my mind's eye, I saw how I was tearing apart the pompous grass-lover in that Dicky Dirt filled with Bhagwan's shit fuckers. A warning that it was not yet time to head back to the fucking ashram. My heart played tam-tam in overdrive. My hands itched. I should have torn his jugular out with my own bleedin' teeth, *I thought,* instead of running away and getting stiff-drunk.

We came onto a big boulevard; I breathed the exhaust of thousands of rickshaws and was close to suffocation when we left the boulevard and drove into a quarter full of rickety houses and narrow alleyways. Laundry was drying on the roofs. We went by a mosque and an open space that was used as a landfill and as an outdoor school. A man stood before a blackboard in the midst of heaps of ordure. Rows of girls with head-scarves sat in the dirt behind him. We roared past; a labyrinth of precarious streets with earth-colored shacks followed. The women leaning against faded posters in these alleys wore micro-skirts in vulgar colors, lowly cut blouses, and no hijab. They wiggled their breasts at me or turned and stooped. The driver stopped, pointed to a house, and said, "Bangla." Two ruminating cows were lying in the dust near the entrance. I got out; a woman ran over and pushed her pelvis against me. "You like me, yes?"

I pushed her away and stumbled into the gray house. I entered a dark, rectangular room where some men, clad in filthy longhi, huddled together. They leered at me with turtle-eyes. At the far end of the room, a fat man, his torso naked and gleaming, sat on a podium. The room stank of piss and strong alcohol. The fat man pointed to a free table. I sat, felt dizzy again. Anger and frustration fished bile up from my stomach. A small boy came with a bottle and a glass. Bangla was a self-distilled, dark fluid flecked with gray patches, not unlike dandruff, leftovers from the fermentation of some ingredients, including chicken innards. The boy filled my glass halfway. I saw it double again, had to try twice before I had it firmly in my right paw. I knocked it down. A firecracker exploded in my stomach, a cramp flogged my body. I gestured to the boy. He filled the glass again and made a pay-up sign with his thumb and forefinger. I gave him ten rupee. He snatched the note from my hand and disappeared.

I don't know how long I sat there, but I remember that my glass was empty again when I stood up and recited the poem I wrote yesterday night in my room.

> *'I just shed my antistatic overalls.*
> *I just threw away my balaclava*
> *I just crammed my asbestos gloves*
> *In the mouth of the machine*
> *that spits fire like lava*
> *I'm naked now like a Levantine*
> *Life still has me by the balls.'*

All the men in the joint applauded.

***

During Alan's story, Johnny's mind had wondered off to a lecture he had attended after he'd left Ma Sarita that day. A gray-bearded *sannyasin* who called himself Swami Prasad, an Italian in his fifties with his hair in a ponytail and an enormous furrow in his disproportionately big chin, had pontificated, "The only love that is worth to induce—and what a gigantic effort it takes!—is self-love. Before you can love yourself, before you can generate this enormous energy, you must explore your periphery, there where the Lords of Pain rule and the Concubines of Fear dominate."

Johnny shook his head, thinking about all the money he had spent and wondering if Alan was right with his assessment of the ashram.

Suddenly, Alan reached out and pulled his nose.

Hard.

***

"Pay attention. I can see you're not listening. You must know what happened to me before you go with me outside. It's important.

When I left the Bangla-joint the bangle outside hit me in force. Children danced around me. Baksheesh, mista, baksheesh! *A drain ran in the middle of the alley, filled with black, shiny slime. I aimed a green blob at it. I heard the call of a Muezzin reverberating in the air; the words were like knives cutting into me. A half naked old man sat rocking his body beside a ridiculous heap of red piccolo caps, humming* ohm ohm ohm.... *Farther down in the alley, I spotted a public latrine. The stench almost knocked me out. Light-rose vapors rose from the shit. I remember thinking: "Where am I? Who am I?"*

And then, I saw it. A dark haired dog with a lame behind dragged himself through the dirt. He saw me looking at him and tried to scurry away; he was so scared that solely the whites of his eyes were visible. I saw his ribs heave fiercely. His fur was missing in many places, and he had red warts everywhere. On his back, an abscess had been ruptured: it oozed a thick yellow fluid.

There and then my heart broke. I don't know why, but out of the blue I felt so much pain in my ticker that my knees buckled. The pain had something to do with my youth; I felt why in a flash, but it vanished before I could recognize its meaning. Did I have a dog when I was a toddler, and was it taken away from me? I will never know, I guess. The images I have from my childhood are exclusively tied to those manifold occasions when my old man unbuckled his belt....

A biblical anger replaced my sorrow. I went after the animal. Groaning, it tried to push itself into the earth; it tried to bite me. I took it in my arms—it was as light as a feather—and I kissed it on the nose. It yelped; I cuddled it. It shivered; I stroked it.

A light descended upon me and I knew I had found a way to open my heart for love. So fast it all went, but so clear, so irrevocable, so definite.

And that's why you must come along. Now. I will show you the real me, the Alan I am deep inside, and I do this because you were kind to me yesterday morning at breakfast. Come with me, Flemish bookstore owner, there is no minute to waste.

17

The night-sky was pristine violet blue; the stars were beige pinpricks. Johnny could hear faint drumming coming from the ashram. Alan led him in the hotel-garden. They passed in silence the circles of Banyan-trees, the carefully constructed and trimmed flower-domes, and the ancient cedars overlooking small, delicately formed ponds.

Sunderban's proprietor was mighty proud of his garden; he would have exploded in fury when he had found the gnarled hound, spreading a distasteful odor, tethered to the great three-stemmed Baobab tree that marked the border of his territory. The animal whimpered as they closed in and tried to get away. Alan made soothing noises, opened his small rucksack and produced leftovers of his dinner. Johnny studied the Londoner while he coaxed the animal to eat something. He also saw the bowl of fresh water nearby. Alan looked over his shoulder. In the beige-bluish skylight, Johnny saw how Alan's face had changed. His lips were relaxed; the sharp lines descending from the sides of his nose to his mouth were less visible. It was a younger, more vulnerable face.

"I had to bind him to the tree, else he would've run. I hope I can set him free when he knows that he can trust me."

Alan's voice carried the tonality of an excited, whispering teenager. The dog sucked and gnawed at a heap of chicken flesh-and-bones. "Listen, Johnny, I know that I'm soused every evening. It has been like that for many years and I don't know if I'll be able to change in a few days. So you must come here in the mornings after breakfast and feed him. Purloin all you can from the buffet in a bag. Let's get him strong again. I can feel that this dog is a soul filled with light that's ready to spread out and touch others. Just look at him: seeing him is loving him." Alan crouched down beside the animal that showed its bleeding gums and bad teeth but continued to wolf down the leftovers. Slowly, he extended his hand. Johnny was sure that Alan would be bitten and prepared himself for the shock when the diseased and infected animal drew blood.

Bob Van Laerhoven

It didn't happen. A few minutes later, the dog was still eating, Alan's right hand slowly caressing its neck. It groaned, barely audible. Alan was so focused on the dog that Johnny had to whisper twice, "Somebody is coming!"

The warning finally registered. The cockney labourer's left hand went into his jacket and produced a *kirpan,* a curved Sikh dagger. The fact that Johnny couldn't see Alan's eyes behind his dark glasses, made him very uncomfortable. Quickly, he put his finger to his lips, and motioned that Alan should stay where he was while he went to take a look.

Alan nodded but made a slashing gesture before his own throat with the sheathed dagger and then pointed in the direction of the noise.

The message was clear.

***

The fat Indian fellowman and his wife were strolling in Johnny's direction when he came from behind the baobab trees. Heaven be praised, their three brats were nowhere in sight.

"Good evening," Johnny said. "Nice garden, isn't it?"

Two puffed up, gleaming faces watched him suspiciously. Since they didn't answer, Johnny felt he had to win time. He indicated a wooden statue of an elephant-like being with many arms that stood in an arbor of violet-flowered bushes.

"Can you please tell me what that is?"

The man frowned, tucked in his chin, and guffawed. "What? Who, you mean! That is the great god Ganesha, the *deva* of wisdom. He wouldn't deign to speak to you, Englishman."

"I'm sorry," Johnny said. "I'm not an English-"

The Indian looked over Johnny's shoulder, and narrowed his eyes. Johnny turned his head. Alan stood in full sight in front of a baobab tree with his fly undone. His urine, etched silver-colored against the night-sky, flew in a wide arc. Johnny noticed that Alan was a large built male, especially on such a tawny frame. Alan saw them looking and turned his pecker in their direction. Again, the message was clear: *come over, fatso, and I'll piss on you.*

The Indian's wife tugged his sleeve.

"Sir!" the Indian thundered.

The dog behind the baobab-screen whined.

"What was that?"

Anger, fear, and impatience took hold of Johnny. *Why me? Why always me?* To his great relief, Alan rushed behind the trees to pamper his dog.

"Please, pardon my…my friend the poet. He is like that sometimes when he's stuck with his writing. He's trying to finish a poem about the sacredness of this garden and the complexity of the Indian pantheon. You will understand that this is not the easiest task, particularly for a Westerner with high literary standards like him." *What am I blabbering? Where does this rubbish come from? Am I becoming insane?*

The woman said something in Hindi to her husband. Johnny had disliked her at first sight: she wore her pot-belly as though it was a passport to superiority. The Indian came closer. Johnny saw crumbs in his beard when he brought his mouth to Johnny's right ear. "You don't fool us with your lies. We know what kind of people you are; perverts like you belong in jail, *samaligī*, both of you." He spat on the grass. "Men who fornicate with men are the lowest beings of Creation." The wife made an ugly sound and twirled her hips obscenely.

"That's not…" Johnny began. Where on Earth did they get the idea that Alan and he were gay?

The duo had already turned around; the husband made a dismissive gesture. "Take my advice, and leave Poona before I warn the police, man-beasts from the third sex!"

Inwardly seething, and also mightily afraid, Johnny returned to Alan and his dog. The Londoner had dozed off; the dog was resting his head in his lap, and sighed contentedly. Alan's left hand still clutched his knife.

"*Zatlap*,*" Johnny hissed. [* Boozer.]

Then he saw that the Sikh dagger was unsheathed and that the blade pointed upward in his direction to his belly region.

18

The night brought Johnny no solution, no absolution, no solace. The night simmered with fear, remorse, murderous fantasies, and suicide impulses.

The room resonated like a huge bell *Why? Why me?*

Johnny pondered the futility of human existence.

He cogitated about the uncontrollability of the human brain.

He ruminated about the folly of human agony.

And, finally, he couldn't think of anything else than of the appointment he had within a few hours with Ma Sarita. The day before she had said it was time for a Left Hand Path Tantric Union. Johnny gawked at the cold that materialized in his feet each time when he imagined how it would be. A squeaky voice, a kind of undercurrent in his mind, insisted monotonously that Ma Sarita was going to let him fuck her like a mad rabbit, a mad rabbit, a mad rabbit.

Just like the FRNB, the Fat Retarded Neighbor Bully, had ravaged him.

The million-dollar question remained: did the FRNB truly exist?

Johnny didn't want to dig for answers anymore. He concentrated on the sensations in his body: a nervous prickling, a mixture of fear and folly, a painfully throbbing groin like a spear into the heart of Christ.

This raw anger.

This ravishing need.

This ravenous fear.

Even for a crippled dog that waited to be fed after breakfast.

I won't feed the mongrel tomorrow morning, I can't do it, I simply cannot, I cannot stand seeing an innocent being suffer like that. Besides, he would bite me, I'm sure.

***

In the middle of the night, Johnny heard psychopathic roaring, yelling voices, crashing furniture.

He stuck his head under his pillow.

19

The Sanderban waiter almost literally threw a plate with two slices of garlic-and-cardamom *naan*—Indian bread—on Johnny's breakfast table. He marched away, his back ramrod straight. Johnny, alone in the eating place, felt his heart sink in his chest.

As on cue, Sanderban's owner came in with martial strides, scowled, and said, "I want you out this evening before five o'clock. You will leave, or the police will arrest you, just like they did last night with your perverted companion. I have always said that the Western followers of the so-called *acharya* Rajneesh are here to fornicate everything that moves."

"What happened?" Johnny managed to say.

"Your 'friend' has been identified as the attacker of an Indian girl yesterday late afternoon during the market on Laxmi road. He tried to hump her like a beast in broad daylight, behind some stalls. He was inebriated, but managed to escape when passersby heard the girl cry and gave chase. Thanks to our dignified police corps, he was identified and arrested this night, here in my hotel. You, sir, brought shame to my esteemed establishment!"

"But I am not in any way connected to Alan…. To this gentleman! He's English and I am—"

"Liar! You told yesterday morning, in this very place, in front of witnesses, that you plan to publish a collection of 'poems' of this pervert!"

"That was…."

"Enough! You will be at my desk before five o'clock, you will pay and you will vanish out of my sight! Am I understood?"

"But…."

Eyes blazing, the owner turned on his heels, and left, swinging his arms like a majorette.

20

"I am a liar, that's a truth I no longer can deny, but I can't remedy it. It just happens. My lies are faster than the truth." Johnny's uptight and chaotic confession was inspired by his hope to reach the promised fucking stage of that day's session as soon as possible. It was all he wanted at that moment. Forget the money. Forget the questions he wished to ask Bhagwan. Forget the huge mistake of coming to Poona. Get out of India, but fuck her first.

"Okay," said Ma Sarita absent-mindedly, although she had just caressed Johnny's dick with nimble, velvet fingers. The session had started promisingly, but then she abruptly had brought up his 'addiction to lying' again. "You must know what fate lies ahead of you if you go on lying." She took a book from the table, consulted the page content, leafed through it, and read aloud, "When a believer utters a lie without a valid excuse, he is cursed by seventy thousand angels. Such a stench emanates from his heart that it reaches the sky. Because of this single lie Allah writes for him a sin equivalent to that of committing seventy hellish fornications, the least of which is fornication with one's mother."

Johnny hesitated between merriness and angriness. "Well well," he said. "Do you believe that?"

She smiled. "Do you?"

"Of course not." He showed his teeth in a poor imitation of a smile. "I'm not a Muslim and I'm not interested in fornications with my mother."

"But you nurse a hidden guilt, the source of all your lies."

Johnny stared at her frowning. She had caught him off-guard; he had been distracted by the Quran *ayat* she just had read.

Ma Sarita saw that her trick worked and knew she had to keep the momentum going.

"You haven't been raped by the retarded neighbor boy, have you?"

For a second, it seemed he was going to punch her in the face. Instead, he shook his head.

It was now or never. If she waited too long, he would hide in his shell again. "But your *Shadow* rapes you every day. I think you know the source of your lying bouts. When you keep denying what you deep down know, the Shadow will keep on disgracing you. He's the one that puts the lies in your mouth. He is the one that lives your life."

Johnny threw his hands before his face.

"Johnny," Ma Sarita said. "Do you realize what I'm saying? *Another one in you is talking; someone other than you lives your life.*"

It was then that Johnny di Machio hissed like a snake. Only the life-long conduct of a coward restrained him by a hair from assaulting her.

She brought her face close to his. "Your lies and your sexual problems are tied together."

"I lie because I am a coward."

"You're not a coward. In you slumbers the courage to recognize your Shadow, or your Golem, if you prefer that name. Otherwise, you wouldn't have come all this way."

"I'm a coward," he repeated stubbornly.

"Then go. Leave your life in the hands of another."

Johnny audibly gnashed his teeth in frustration. Everything that had happened these last days seemed to drive him to an uncontrollable, long hidden fury. Glowing pin-pricks of light appeared in his field of vision and turned into black dots. Was his blood-pressure going manic? He remembered the *sannyasin* Arup's remark about a dark presence in his mind. His mother once had said that he was born almost suffocated by the birth membrane still tight around his head.

He felt suffocated now.

Ma Sarita touched the small bell at her right hip. She was taking a considerable risk. She also knew she was very close.

"Your golem must be laughing in your face," she said. "Isn't it time to *do* something?"

His face became red, his features distorted, his eyes bulged. She should ring now. *Now.*

She didn't, and all of a sudden Johnny collapsed on his yoga-mat and retched as if he was going to throw up.

"He did it," he stammered, his voice strangled and high-pitched, the voice of a very frightened boy. "I lied all the time, but *it happened.* He did it."

She bent and embraced him. His skin felt feverish.

"Who did what? Tell me. You're safe. Set yourself free, Johnny."

"Lard-man did it," Johnny whispered, not realizing that he used the nick-name his thirteen-year-old neighbor Rocco had in his village twelve years ago.

A dam in him broke. The story of Lard-man left his mouth, just like all his lies earlier in his life: before he fully realized it.

21

Lard-man, hey, Lard-man, show us your Lard-dick!

Rocco was flattered when my friends and I urged him to roll down his pants and underpants on market-day in our village, so that we could delight in the shrieks of the market-women. His broad, Mongolian-like face lighted up like a candle. "Lard! Lard!" he jubilated.

In 1964, ours was a small village with just one elder gardevil—a deputy-sheriff—who generally came running over too late and shouted amiably, "Com'on, Rocco, stuff your thingy away, or I'll shoot it right in the, ehh, head!"

The gardevil got his reward: the market-women laughed even harder than they had shrieked.

Oh well, the boy suffered from Down-syndrome and was retarded, wasn't he? And boys will be boys. Maybe, Rocco would be better off in an institution, but, Lord, his poor mother, married to the only garage keeper in the village, would scratch the eyes out of everyone who dared to take her thirteen-year-old son away from her.

Rocco was the humming mascot of the woods that surrounded our village, the eternal smiling Buddha of the wheat fields, and the magnanimous white whale of our river that carried with great pride the name Campinaria Canal, centuries ago given to it by Roman invaders.

Rocco was also Mr. Coca Cola bottle dick and could get hard at will.

Even on the market-place, if the gardevil *wasn't around.*

The market-women wailed harder than ever when Rocco's rigid rod exposed itself in all its glory, and we, adolescents, whispered to each other they did it out of envy.

***

Evening, July 1964.

I was reading "Winnetou and the Gold-diggers," a Western by the German novelist Karl May in the riverweeds between the poplars that lined Campinaria's basin. Winnetou and Old Shatterhand were a hundred carat real heroes. Unlike me, they always forgave their enemies.

The basin was shallow and sandy. The weeds between the trees grew about 150 cm. tall, an ideal place to change clothes. Girls went in groups there to dress after swimming; boys one after one.

The day had been hot and moist; now, a fair amount of cumulus was playing hide-and-seek with the sun.

Nobody was swimming in the basin when I'd arrived. I would become thirteen that summer. A peculiar loneliness possessed me since months, a void I couldn't understand.

At some point, I must have fallen asleep with my face on my book. When I woke up, I heard splashing noises. I peered through the riverweeds, and saw Gaby-of-Copper swimming in the basin, fourteen-year-old Gaby with her flame-colored hair, her delicate body, and her doe-like eyes.

Everybody called her Gaby-of-Copper, not for her hair but for the copper colored big birthmark on her left leg. A loner she was, Gaby. I thought I knew why she was swimming when she thought no-one else was around. A few months ago, at the terrace of Café bij Jeanne *where the adolescents of our village were welcome to drink their first beer when there were no adults in the rustic joint, a local bully by the nick-name of Headbutt Danny had lashed out to mini-skirted Gaby, "Oh-ho-ho-ho, Gabyke? What do I see, poor me? D'ye have the runs? Did ye shit your panties and forgot to wipe yur leg?" No laughter, absolute silence. Gaby didn't answer. She turned around and left. Her yellow, almost see-through miniskirt danced around her shapely buttocks and the big birthmark on her left leg resembled a shard of copper, sharp enough to cut off your fingers.*

***

I was still spying on Gaby when she came out of the water. Drops reflected on her body with a golden shine. I felt a stirring in my groin, a pressure like a sudden push in the back. I remember it to this day as a longing to be a sorcerer who could make her crawl on her knees and do everything he wanted.

From thereon, my memory is hazy. Something felt wrong in my head for a while, as if there had been a time-jump; I feel onto this day the residue of aches and pangs behind my eyes. Everything around me seemed elongated, surrounded by bizarre shadows and blazing pools of light in Campinaria's water.

It was a world in which Golems dwelled.

I know it's impossible, but the memory is right here, etched in my mind: out of nowhere, I saw Rocco charging out of the bushes and racing to the river's bank, his hands held high, totally naked, his potbelly wiggling, his Coca Cola bottle-dick swaying. He literally ran Gaby-of-Copper over. Before I realized what was going on, Rocco's dough-white body lay on top of Gaby. He tried to push his way in with his Coca Cola bottle. I heard Gaby-of-Copper scream. I saw her wrestle him. I saw Rocco's milk-white ass wriggle between her legs.

And then, all of a sudden, Rocco sang. I swear to God I heard him sing. Rocco was known to sing when he was excited. We young guys, secretly afraid of him, used to tell each other that his singing came from the frog king within him, sounds that, in our imagination, Indian tribes yodeled during rituals to call on the spirits. It went like this: hmmmmm-ooooo-ouuuuu-hi-hi-hay-yah-hmmmmm-huhuhuhu ha yay...

I could see the frog king taking possession of Rocco, and how he moved inside Gaby-of-Copper; I could hear her cries, and my hands and feet turned into ice.

I crept backwards to where my bike laid, my heart a drum in my throat. Without looking over my shoulders, I pedaled away from there as if an old, hungry beast of the forest and the water was chasing me.

22

Johnny swam in the Endless Sea of Satisfaction; he didn't panic; he didn't get soft inside her like so often before with the alter-egos of Gaby-of-Copper he had bedded.

Ma Sarita looked him straight in the eye; Johnny felt the urgency of an important message there. His heart wept, his eyes remained dry, captured in the spell of her gaze.

The message became loud and clear.

Exorcize the past. Do it now. Sing.

***

A few days later, Rocco was taken away by force to an institution, never to be seen again in our village. His mother divorced soon after and went living in Antwerp. I often saw Gaby-of-Copper when I biked to school. Our eyes never met, but every time my heart fluttered and then wept in my chest.

If I had been Winnetou, I would've saved her, would've slinked closer and hit Rocco on the head with a stone.

If I had been Old Shatterhand, I would've crept closer and lassoed Rocco with a noose around his neck.

I ran.

I was a coward.

***

Ma Sarita contracted her belly muscles, then her perineum, as was the ritual in *The Left Hand Path of Tantra*. She whispered *Gehe finstere Wolke*—leave, sinister cloud—in Johnny's ear. Like any true Fleming, son of a father who had been in the resistance in WWII, Johnny could speak German more or less and understood what she said, but his mind drowned in waves of nerve-fire, and the only thing he answered was : *hmmmmm-ooooooouuuuu-hi-hi-hay-yah-hmmmmm-huhuhuhu ha yay...*

When Johnny realized what he was doing, an ominous urge of

possession, pure malfeasance, rode on the fire-breathing horse that invaded his body. It was the demon that had possessed Rocco. Johnny flayed his arms and pounded his pelvis against Ma Sarita's body. She didn't flinch and met him thrust for thrust, her eyes boring in his.

Sing.

He started to hum again, and this time, with Rocco's song, came the tears that filled his eyes. *Hmmmmm-oooooouuuuu-hi-hi-hay-yah-hmmmmm-huhuhuhu ha yay...*

As abruptly as it had come, the dark cloud that enveloped him was gone, and Johnny felt undiluted love. His heart received a soft blow, as if a piece of it had been missing for so long, and now had been put back with a gentle pat.

"I'm going to come," he whispered.

Waves of angry human noises spread over the ashram as a tsunami, followed by cries of fear and pain.

Ma Sarita pushed Johnny off her, ran to the entrance of the tent, looked outside, turned, shouted "run," snatched her robe from a chair and pulled it over her head.

23

Never had Johnny seen such a crowd of angry men with maddened eye-whites. They streamed into the ashram and destroyed everything in their path. Johnny saw the haughty *sannyasin* flee like rabbits. He did so too.

He had one advantage over Bhagwan's followers: he didn't wear his orange robe. That morning, confused and angry after the Sanderban's owner chiding, he had left the hostel and realized he didn't wear his robe at the entrance of the ashram. Too late to turn back; he would've missed his appointment with Ma Sarita. After explaining the situation to the sentry, he received a reprimand but had been allowed inside.

Johnny bounded like a hare over the terrains. He hadn't bothered to put on his underpants and in his haste to dress he wore his T-shirt inside out. However, the seething mass of Indians was focused on orange, and soon Johnny saw his chance to dodge unchallenged through the commune's exit.

Outside, to his left, he saw more people running to the entrance. He turned right and walked away, his back muscles a bone-hard knot of fear.

Farther down the road, the fracas dying away behind him, he realized he couldn't remember if Ma Sarita had still been in her tent when he ran off. Had she escaped before him or did she stay behind, paralyzed by fear?

His mind's eye pictured her, raped by hordes of Indian rabble, choking on their sperm.

They got it all, those execrable Indians, the fizzle and the lava, the belly-dragon and the phoenix, while he, unsanctified swami Johnny-yoki from Flanders, had been so close, so nigh, to at long last hit the high spot.

24

The prison-guard pointed at one of the rows of hut-like cells of the open-air prison, muttered "number three," and left Johnny abruptly. The atmosphere in the prison reminded Johnny more of a military training centre than a prison. The khaki-clad guards were idling around, and prisoners walked between the huts, involved in heated discussions. Then he saw that the iron-barred doors of some cell-rows were open and some were not. The row which the guard had appointed had closed doors.

Johnny walked over and peered inside hut number three. At least ten prisoners were packed in the small interior. Alan slumped in a corner. The heat inside the cell was suffocating. Johnny saw that Alan didn't wear his glasses. In the beer-colored light, his bulging, ice-blue left eye-ball transformed him into a creature of nightmares. When he saw Johnny, he came to the door, dodging pushes and blows, and gripped the bars so hard that his knuckles went ice-white.

"Don't ask me anything about what happened," he said in a low voice. "Don't dare to ask."

Johnny stared at him dumbfounded.

"Don't you understand? They would—a swift pantomime of throat cutting—if they knew why I'm in here for. Talk about the dog. Don't talk about me."

"The dog?"

"My dog, for god's sake. In the garden. Did you feed him this morning?"

Johnny nodded.

"What did you give him?"

"Part of my English breakfast: sausages, meats, bacon and such, boiled eggs." Johnny felt lead in his feet. Clearer than ever before, he felt that indeed *someone else* spoke instead of him, *someone else* led his life. Why else had he come to say goodbye to this would-be rapist who had caused him nothing but trouble? To tell Alan that he would have been able to come in Ma Sarita's luscious body if the ashram hadn't been invaded as a result of Alan's stupid brazenness?

Alan nodded. "You're a good guy, Johnny."

"Can I do anything more for….the dog?" Johnny smelled an open latrine nearby and thought pathetically: *that's the stench of my soul.*

Alan looked at him dubiously. "Why do you ask?"

"I must leave Poona this evening."

Alan closed his eyes and rested his forehead on the bars. "Who will tend to my dog then?"

"I….don't know."

"Can't you *do* something for that poor creature? You can't leave it there to wither away!"

"It's…."

"I've felt it, I tell you, Johnny, I've felt it crystal-clearly: that dog is a pure soul. He deserves a good life." Alan was breathing heavily, as though he was on the verge of an asthma attack. "I'm garbage, don't think I don't realize that, but he's…he's….*pure.*"

Johnny surmised that large quantities of *bangla* had damaged Alan's brain. The dog was a goner; that was for sure. The mutt couldn't even walk decently, and god knows what contagious diseases it harbored.

"Please," Alan said. "Please help him, help my poor dog."

It struck Johnny that Alan didn't ask for help for himself. He found himself staring at the ugly misshapen left eyeball. *Could it be that even this troglodyte is a better man than I am?*

"Maybe I can take him to a…. a vet, where he can be treated… until you get free…"

Alan brightened. "Yes! Do that. They can take care of him until I'm free. That shouldn't take long. Tomorrow, somebody of the embassy is coming. There are witnesses of the whole sordid affair, but nothing really happened. Nothing *could've* happened either. I was blitzed about from that hooch bangle. There's no *proof.* Tell the vet that he has to do everything to patch my dog up, the best food and the best care. I'll settle the bill as soon as I can pick him up. Don't forget to stress that it is very important that the poor sod is treated well."

Johnny nodded, taken aback by the hope in Alan's voice.

"Do it right away, wouldn't you, mate? Bring him in safety."

"Okay, okay... I'll...I'll leave the vet's address at the entrance of the...the jail."

"Please, Johnny, give the vet an advance and leave behind the number of your bank account in Sanderban. I swear that I'll wire you the money when I am out of here. You have my word."

"Eh...Okay. I'll do that."

Alan literally beamed now. "I always thought you were a great guy. Do you really have to leave?"

"I....I've booked a bus ticket to Goa....Some friends of mine are there...waiting for me...I have to go now, Alan, I still have to pack and to...arrange everything for the dog."

"I understand, brother. Mine is fucked up, but I wish you the best life possible. I could've been different, you know, if....Things happened when I was very young, and they made me, well... angry and sad." Alan gave a right-hand thud on his chest. "There's so much here, inside, you know. So much...But that doesn't concern you, not your business."

"I hope everything will turn for the good for you." In a sudden flash of intuition, Johnny added. "You need a compassionate woman in your life, Alan."

The street-fighter's Adam's apple went up and down a few times.

"Come a bit closer," Alan mumbled.

Reflexively, thinking that Alan wanted to share a secret, Johnny stepped forward. Alan's right arm circled Johnny's neck and drew his head to the bars. A prickly kiss, swift as a snake-bite, on his cheek, and Johnny, blushing profusely, was released.

"Is there...anything more that I can do?"

"Just provide for my dog, mate, don't forget to leave the vet's address and your bank account number."

"I won't. Bye now, Alan."

"Bye, brother. Wish you the best. *You're* the best."

On his way to the jail's exit, marked by a sickle-shaped, violet board full of undecipherable Hindi signs, Johnny had to fight for breath. His pumped-up heart seemed wired to rip his chest apart.

Why am I always doing everything wrong?

25

In the taxi on the way to Bangalore, the Hindi pop-music that had been droning for hours became a screeching mumbo-jumbo, accompanied by static. The driver, who had presented himself as Mr. Anwar, turned the dial and after minutes of hissing, a clear voice filled the speakers.

Bhagwan's voice.

The driver turned around and announced proudly: "All India Radio is the largest radio network in the world!"

Johnny signaled him to turn the volume up. The driver complied.

"…What gives a British visitor of my ashram the audacity to harangue an Indian woman on our market-place? Surely, you can answer that question for yourself. The man is *British*. His ego is his own personal enemy, while he thinks it is his greatest power. I am a bell that tolls *Awaken, awaken, awaken,* but ego-driven people are stone-deaf. To be awake means that one has to live in the *now*. Ego-driven people don't have that special kind of patience; they live in the future, in the past, in their ego-fed dreams, in whatever dimension, but not in the *now*. The ego is mankind's main neurosis, and some suffer more than others. Ego-driven people become sooner or later a danger to others and themselves, devoid from love as they are. I am only a conduit for the mystery of love; I cannot and will not explain it. But I'll tell you this: everything around us is an illusion, created by ego. Only real love can shatter that illusion. But real love is a condition that is extremely hard to reach. It's a bigger mystery than life, because what we call life is not life alone, but life plus death. You can only feel real love when you're prepared to die. The Englishman, the rapist, as you call him, obviously cannot know what real love is and as long—"

Mr. Anwar turned with an impatient gesture the dialing knob. Johnny wanted to object, but kept his mouth shut. It had started to rain intensely and the old Tara-taxi had only one working windscreen wiper. It had become dark and the road swept precipitously upwards. Johnny had seen several wrecks in ravines on the way.

"Rajneesh is solely good for weaklings," the driver said. "Hindu people and Westerners are his prey. We Muslim don't need such charlatans."

"You don't think he's a holy guru, like many people do?"

Mister Anwar looked condescendingly at Johnny in his mirror.

"Holiness is definitely not the background of Rajneesh's 'religion'," he said. "On the contrary." He put his hand on his crotch and moved a flaccid index finger. "*Fuck no possible.*"

A violent bump, followed by an uncanny howling.

"What was that?"

Mr. Anwar looked over his shoulder, showed Johnny lots of eye-white, but didn't answer. Johnny turned his head but he couldn't see far with the rain and the dark road. He thought he saw something moving in the mud.

"Was that a dog howling? Did you crash into a dog?"

Again, the driver shrugged.

Johnny felt a numbness creeping to his knees.

What could I have done? I didn't have enough money left to care for that dog. Alan will have forgotten about him by now. Drunks are like that. The mutt is probably dead already. His suffering is over.

Johnny blinked; he felt a lump in his throat. *Alan is a better man than I am. He sincerely loved the mongrel.*

The remorse that made him shiver was as intense as the guilt that had plumped upon him when he ran away from Rocco and Gaby-of-Copper, the two-headed monster that writhed on the banks of the river.

It was also as big as the lorry that descended, its engine droning like a Mad Max-vehicle, from the mountain road, hurtling straight at Mr. Anwar's Tata.

OTHER
ANAPHORA LITERARY
PRESS TITLES

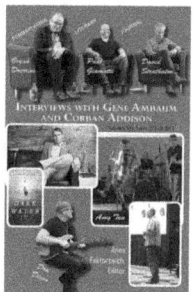

PLJ: Interviews with Gene Ambaum and Corban Addison: VII:3, Fall 2015
Editor: Anna Faktorovich

Architecture of Being
By: Bruce Colbert

The Encyclopedic Philosophy of Michel Serres
By: Keith Moser

Forever Gentleman
By: Roland Colton

Janet Yellen
By: Marie Bussing-Burks

Diseases, Disorders, and Diagnoses of Historical Individuals
By: William J. Maloney

Armageddon at Maidan
By: Vasyl Baziv

Vovochka
By: Alexander J. Motyl

Lightning Source UK Ltd.
Milton Keynes UK
UKHW01f1845041018
329996UK00001B/195/P